THE ESSENCE OF LONELINESS

IDA STARK

Ida Stark
Alingsås

@idyllienodyssey
idyllienodyssey@gmail.com

Publisher: BoD – Books on Demand, Stockholm, Sweden
Print: BoD – Books on Demand, Norderstedt, Germany
ISBN: 978-91-8027-530-9

To Ingrid and Rune; the goodness in my life.

I am floating in a pink sphere, levitating in the universe; it is cold, and no sign of life as far as my scenes reach. Only me— I am happy. Only me—I am free. Never again will I be tortured. I've left earth traveling towards new goals; towards what humanity called love, ethics, and morals. Even if there is no air—my lungs are full. Even if there is no other soul—I feel love. I now know what awaits me after all these years of pain; there could be nothing left but pure love.

1. OUR MEETING

I never asked for a man to marry,
nor to be the woman you adore.
All I want is to become seen
—as a person.
With all my beauty,
all of my flaws.

He had already planned it. He always planned his actions; even so, he was not someone who wouldn't grab an opportunity when it presented itself. Since he was a man of many ideas, opportunities often presented themselves. What made him the most successful was that he would listen and learn. Sometimes he didn't even know how he did it; he didn't have the time to understand all of his thoughts fully. He had a feeling based on all the information he processed, which was accurate most of the time. *This ability was what made me rich*, he thought to himself and smirked. When he wanted to do something, he just found a way of doing it. Ever since he was young, he had known that knowledge brings power, even though it could also bring a lot of pain when you present it to others—if they didn't like it.

He observed her across the room; she had not seen him yet. In the periphery, he saw people moving, hearing the sound of coworkers laughing and porcelain mugs clocking. Thinking to himself, *why are we so obsessed when in love?* He couldn't help himself from smiling. He could not see her enough, this feeling he had before with other girls when he was young and with his previous wife as well. Even if he knew that at some point, the obsessive feeling towards her would go away, he decided that he would let himself enjoy it while it lasted. This time he couldn't get the sense out of his head that it could be different; *she was different*—or so his dopamine-filled brain thought. It was some sort of connection he felt with her that he wasn't sure he had before. He never really longed to have sex with just any girl, even if he had tried that too. For him to feel really attracted, there had to be something special that caused his attention—a connection. Their coworkers often considered her a peculiar woman as they spent time together. The way she would laugh at his jokes, humor that generally only a few of his friends would get, made him feel close to her. When she made the mark even wittier, he could not help himself from laughing but also thinking to himself; *she gets me.* He felt as though maybe, he could love her—not that he really thought so. He had a hard time telling someone he loved them; he thought himself to forgotten how love felt—if he'd ever known. Whatever love means. It was not the same for him as it seemed for those he believed he loved. He considered that the love he had for his kids might have to be enough for him. He would always try and give them all he thought would be good for them; to show his appreciation for having them in his life. Experience told him that in relationships, it was never that simple.

The lunchroom cleared except for her; he walked up to her, asking her to join him for dinner that evening. She smiled at him as if she could hear him screaming *yes!* In his head when she gave him the answer. He already knew she would say yes. His gut told him so. She excused herself avidly, being in a hurry. Before she was about to exit the room, she turned her head to look at him, to get a last glimpse before leaving. Her eyes glistened with curiosity and excitement. He couldn't bear the feeling of wanting to feel her skin, thinking of her naked body in his bed—then try something new he had thought about doing. He was a man who made his dreams come true, and so would his plans with her; he knew it.

Later that day, he dressed himself up for their dinner. *Looking like a gentleman,* he thought to himself, giving off a snorting noise. Dressing up gave him the feeling as if he was acting. The clothing had a particular uplifting scent, filling him with excitement. His brain connected the smell to the thrilling events that usually followed. When he was young, he'd never cared much for his clothing. The more he spent time with people who made settling decisions he understood the meaning of dressing fancy. He smiled when he thought about how he sarcastically called them *the decision-makers.* Dressing neatly made him seem more empowered and comfortable when making hard decisions. He taught himself the social coding of how to be; what clothing to wear, what girls he should date—whom he should love. He always hated that game. He hated to judge others by their first look; knowingly, it often said much about people. Some people carried their wisdom hidden, and they would intrigue him. Everyone around him took him and his work so seriously. People couldn't understand how he did it. The truth was he didn't take anything that seriously; he just did it because he wanted to— apparently looking powerful doing so. But tonight was all about having fun and getting her swept away. As he had made the last adjustment to his hair, he looked at himself in the mirror, having no doubt in mind.

She arrived just on time for dinner. Or maybe some minutes late. Even if it was important for her to be on time, she seldom seemed to be these days. She saw him sitting at the table. She fumbled off her bag, tipping over the chair she tried to hang it on. An hour before, she was calm and had her confidence on top, but all the stress from leaving her kids protesting with their dad made her late and twitchy. It used to be so much easier being on time before she had kids; the smoothly sophisticated lady she previously imagined to be was gone. He was soon about to help her get settled on her chair; she felt by his humble look, his smile as he helped her, how much he enjoyed seeing her. He was always happy to help. She excused herself:

"I am glad I have my kids to blame; otherwise, I wouldn't have any good excuses."

"You often kid about things that you actually reckon to be the truth," he said, as she felt his eyes absorbing her to study her reaction. His comment made her thoughts wander for a moment. It was true; some had indicated something like that before but never in the way he had said it. When he said it, she could feel the close observation he had made. It made her feel as if he saw her in a way no one had seen her in a long time. It was an unsettling feeling. Most of the time, she felt as if she played a part of being like everyone else; a part of her longed to be herself—free to speak. She didn't know how others kept their mouths shut; could they not see what she saw? She envied those who always seemed to speak their mind; she often did herself, but all too often—it ended up in misunderstandings. She hated to become misunderstood. He was one of those who often spoke his mind; their conversation entered the subject as the waiter discreetly presented the menu. Caught up in their conversation, they continued talking.

"It is exhausting that they can say that I am rude and impolite, but I can't tell them the truth about their behavior when they make mistakes or fail to see the whole picture," he said as he tossed his head, rolling his eyes.
"Well yeah, if you want them as friends," she said with a certain sarcasm.
"I never want them as friends" his eyes were daring.
"And here we are," she replied, looking at him. Both of them were smiling like they understood one another. It was not that they didn't like other people;

it was just exhausting that society never seemed to get it. Knowingly this was how others sometimes felt about them—they didn't get it. Even if some might consider him odd or emotionally distant, he would feel deeply for those disfavorably treated by society's rules. Those who wished no harm, trying to contribute; yet still ended up mistreated and misunderstood by ordinary people. For him, it was necessary to point out mistreatment when he saw it; others would sometimes consider him arrogant when doing so. He would get provoked by their way of repeating their behavior according to everyone else's. At times he would try to hold his thoughts to himself and adjust to their way of thinking, but it was hard dealing with the feeling of being false.

"I guess that I am a bit too rational for their taste. I just hate when I feel forced to pretend not to see better solutions", his voice was engaged, "it always takes such time cooperating with others when I have to explain my ideas. I guess I am more cut out for the leading role, to explain in a way they sort of understand and then lead. Or maybe just to be on my own." She noticed that this was something that had been bothering him. It connected her to a feeling of isolation, a feeling she would experience in the middle of a group of people, especially when holding back. She gave him a playful reply:

"Oh, admit it! You just love making people uncomfortable! So do I. The way I see it is that I wish to awaken the feeling of them questioning themselves, not to make them feel stupid, more a way to make them snap out of their narrow way of thinking." She never said it like that to anyone before; she didn't quite know why she now did. Looking at him, she felt by his amusement that he understood her intention. What others considered provocative behavior was something that felt right—likely because of her way of being provoked by their way of thinking inside the box.

Their conversation moved on in a rapid phase, unlike how they finished the food they ordered that was now in front of them, unbothered by how the steam that kept rising would decrease the heat and flavor of the dish. He made an honest joke regarding his previous relationship; he now didn't know who to find someone to keep by his side for the rest of his life.
"But you can never keep anyone by your side," she pointed out, "you want them to stay with you because you love them, right? Then you can never persuade them to stay nor ask them never to leave you. You cannot force love because you cannot force someone's genuine interest. You can never keep someone their whole life; only give them as much love as you can—

if you feel like it, and be grateful for the time you get." When she finished speaking, her eyes wandered, looking through the window next to them; seemingly lost in her thoughts.

"So I should just give up on finding someone to stay with me?" It was not a serious question; he thought before he had said it. As he said it aloud, he heard that he actually meant it.

"No, but never let the fear of them leaving you be in control of how you treat them; that's all—be aware of it." She still looked away.

"So young, and you still had time to think about this?" He tried to ease the mood—it did not work. She remained silent, "it stresses me that people seem to leave me. I guess it is true that it would sometimes cause me to push them", he said honestly.

"It was hard for me to understand love because love is not something to learn and understand by yourself. It is supposed to be something you feel with others, the essence of our goodness seen through the eyes of each other. I've forever lost someone I shared my life with for a long time. You know it is impossible to love someone without time spent; without time spent, it becomes more of an adoration. Love is memory, the composure in our bodies in the presence of someone, based on the memories with them. Without these shared memories, it becomes only an admiration—a crush. Even though I did what I could to save my friend, I wish I had been more grateful during the time we shared. Now we can't share any more moments; the memories are starting to fade away. I cannot relive our love for each other; a part of life is fading away, a part of what was our life together." He felt her sorrow and grief through the look in her eyes as she told him; it had him thinking about his own loss.

Many events had hurt him over the years, but nothing hurt him as much as his tremendous deprivation. The loss of his baby girl, who was supposed to be his first genuine love. Someone who would have his infinite adoration. His firstborn child who would be a part of how he knew he wanted a family to be like; a family unlike anything the one in which he grew up—it was now a long time ago. Time has its way of healing the devastation after a loss. Thinking about losing his baby made him remember his inquisitiveness when learning astrophysics while growing up. It helped him to suffer through all the horror he saw as a kid; by understanding where we come from—exploring the boundaries of his imagination. Through books and movies, he found hope for a better future, hope that things didn't have to stay the way they were. In his mind, he would imagine a place of peace where he felt calm, a place of harmony. He often found himself thinking about space when visiting this place of emotional alleviation. It made him feel closer to those whom he had lost. Imagining their existence as a part of this universe made him feel as if they could still be close; no matter in what order, particles that previously created their bodies now had become arranged. Or as if he could exceed his existence and travel to a parallel universe in which he'd never lost them. Both of them had been quiet for a while. The waiter removed their plates, trying to catch their attention but soon moved on when feeling the intense aura surrounding them. Later, when presented with the checkbook, they seemed to snap back from their minds. Without a further plan, they paid and collected their belongings, leaving the restaurant together.

"You have an exceptional mind; why don't you join me for a walk and take care of your brain that I like so much?" She said with a tease and gave him a temptable look, "I like to learn more about your ideas; they intrigue me." For long, they had been seated, caught by their conversation. She seemed to enjoy leaving the indoors, walking into the pouring rain. He looked at her, not wanting to get himself all wet. The rain was falling and turning the street into a stream.

She looked at him with a smile that dared him to follow her; he could not resist her temptation. Never.

"How is it that I feel as though you know me?" He asked as they started walking. Her feet were skipping, seemingly to be almost caught in a dance. She answered him with a smile. He got caught by how she looked at him, eyes that seemed so familiar, yet they had only known each other for a short amount of time. The way she spoke about her feelings was so similar to the way he felt; when he tried talking about his feelings, people would misinterpret them. He felt as if they often told his feelings to be wrong—or at least they seldom seemed to understand them. Even though he had difficulty genuinely connecting with anyone, he realized that there would be others who felt like him. Over the years, he thought himself to have a connection with some of those he had met, but in the end, he often felt as though everyone betrayed him. As if the things they talked about didn't mean the same to them as they did to him. He often felt as though they left him; he knew he had an issue dealing with people going. It was hard to realize that their good time together would not come again the same way it previously had. Whenever given a chance in any relationship, he always tried his best to make it work, yet he always ended up with the same feeling. At times he found himself struggling with feeling alone—abandoned. He felt esteem towards how she seemed never to judge him, but then there were also her eyes, saying so much more. They said she shared his pain and knew what he had been through, but could that possibly be true? Was it all in his head? Was it just the thrill of their whole experience that got to him?

Their clothing was now much heavier than before; some raindrops still fell upon them. Their clothing was dripping as they walked through the city. It had him thinking about the times he'd played with his kids in the rain. Parenting had been challenging for him; to maintain his patience by accepting their inability to control their tantrums, accepting his limitation to prevent his tantrums with them—something he could otherwise handle well. He learned to understand what he felt and communicate that to his children for them to feel safe and become able to do the same. He appreciated spending time with his kids and friends. They whom he now had chosen to have in his life showed him acceptance for who he was—even if they did not always understand him.

"We will always hurt our children, in one way or another, won't we? They will grow up and hopefully learn from our mistakes; if we are lucky—in time, they will understand. Otherwise, only blame us and hold us responsible, I guess. But no one is without mistakes, right? If we didn't fail, we would know how to succeed; that's how humans work." When he'd said it, he noticed how her eyes were focused on the ground as they continued walking. Looking down, she smiled and nodded. Spending time with her kids was one of the things she loved the most; as they spent their time learning, she also learned so much. They had her practice explaining the world in a simplicity that they could understand, in a way that she also had to reformulate her understanding. To observe herself and understand her behavior in order to explain it to them; connecting what is hard to understand with what is easy to understand—how it is all connected. She had always felt that there lay a certain beauty about expressing what seemed to be hard to understand in a simple matter. His words had impacted her; one thing she had to accept as a parent was the constant failure. There is merely not enough time or energy to analyze and make the best decision in every situation; sometimes, you have to fling it. Sometimes, you end up crying yourself when you are to be the one comforting. When she felt as if she couldn't pull through, crying and feeling helpless, she couldn't be prouder than when her kids came and hugged her. All that she hoped for was that they felt the same way when she comforted them. She replied to what he'd said with a humble voice:

"Yeah, I agree, the hard part is not being a parent per see; it is the combination of being a good parent and trying to be the person you want to be with them. The combination of taking care of the rest expected of you in life, different commitments, responsibilities, and weighing them all." They continued to share their experiences on the matter. Darkness was now surrounding them; their walk seemed to have taken them away from the city lights. Above them, the night sky had cleared. Faraway worlds in the form of starlight now unfolded their existence. Down on earth, they continued walking—caught in each other's minds.

As their conversation moved on, it became clear that they shared a fundamental understanding regarding how one should care for other people; also affecting them as parents. Both of them had divorced; for him, it had been short and intense once he had expressed his feelings. For her, it had been an internal struggle over time. She told him about it:

"I know it was hard for my husband, but what else could I do? My husband was a man of hate and anger; these are powerful feelings if you let them be. During our conversations, I was told that my husband would never let go of the hate. My husband thought to be in the right to show hate, seemingly unable to deal with the emotions following our break up—processing our emotions by talking to me. Instead, my husband decided to see me as cruel, withholding the same perspective regardless of my feelings. All because of the alternative; accepting my right to my emotions—my need to be loved and appreciated. My husband could never truly see my beauty and strength nor comfort me when making mistakes; it became clear that my husband never even knew me. I guess it made it hard for me to trust someone again, afraid that it would end up like that again, threats and spiteful words." She felt her sorrow creeping back as she told him, even though she thought herself having dealt with it. "I asked my husband to treat me as a person, not as a woman to keep; it was not possible because of who my husband was—the way my husband perceived me. Some tried to push me towards hate and that we had nothing to do with each other. In my heart, I couldn't bring myself to hate my husband, no matter how much hate that became expressed towards me. What would be the point of hating? We shared so much, and no matter what I felt, I was still me, the same person who cared for my husband. Together we had been through so much. My husband was still the one who had been by my side all these years. We still shared good memories but never spoke the same language. That was what hurt me the most; accepting that we had never had an understanding—I had been living my own lie."

"Yeah, we never really know what's on someone else's mind." He replied with a sympathetic voice, recognizing himself in her feelings.

For him, it wasn't until everything had become torn apart from what once had been their life that he could fully comprehend that they never had an understanding of each other. His wife would not care to understand what he felt when he tried to explain it —or maybe his wife just couldn't understand. He had a hard time accepting that his wife wouldn't hear him. It all felt like a battle; when it was all over, all assets had been shared—no one had won anything. Everyone involved lost, all because they couldn't understand each other. He would never have expected them to end up like that; how it was impossible to resolve all that had become broken between them. He suddenly noticed how far they had gotten. The cold fresh smell awoke him; without mentioning anything, he had them take a turn leading them back to the city.

She didn't reflect on his change in course, caught in memories of the past. She told him about how she tried to survive through the sorrow when she had left her marriage, abandoning almost all material possessions:

"I had to choose what was important to survive; all the objects are just part of a facade. Some I might need, and some might inspire me, but the rest only keep me distracted from being myself. The more I got, the more I brought, more of which I had to care for. I hired people to take care of it, but then I had to manage the ones I hired. I had to make sure everything would run smoothly, or at least didn't decay. My focus was always somewhere else; it kept me from being free to think about what I wanted—to dream. It kept me from being present when spending time with my kids; there is no time but the present for them. There were so many things I had to take care of; at the end of the day, my brain was still working, processing all that was going on—I was never really there." As she said it, she remembered how liberating it felt when she finally left all that was insignificant behind—all those who were insignificant. Her now freezing body had her thinking about the present again, noticing how soaked they both were. She realized that it was probably not the best decision to walk this far in the rain, but none of them cared much for such formalities. Once caught in someone's mind, you are to enjoy the exploration while it happens, or you will forever lose the opportunity.

He processed her words in his head; they gave him new perspectives, shading light some musings he had.
"I haven't thought about it like that, but you are right. In essence, there are two things, abstractions, we need to live our lives and achieve our goals. One is money that lets us use the resources we need; more money means greater, more advanced projects and an easier way to achieve them. With less money, you can still make it happen, but you might have to work harder to make your ideas more efficient; you might also have to use more time to explain yourself to investors or others you need to achieve your goal. Leading to the second one, which is time, time is always a factor; how much time do you have to make it happen? How much do you need to change your time working for others to get the money to make it happen? How much time do you have to gather the information you need? I enjoy my money; still, it is no fun without any time, as you said—to do what I want. Luckily I want to work with what I do, so I get both." He knew sometimes was considered smug to say it; many people would give him condescending looks when he

told them. For him, this was the truth—live by rules. "Even as a boy, I was puzzled regarding time; back then, I lacked the knowledge that I would not be able to learn and do all I wanted—I have to decide what matters. Young and without understanding this, I would go into many projects. It gave me experience, but now I only focus on what matters to me. The things I do, work or other projects, I do because I want to. I think people telling you that you can't do as you feel do so because they don't always go with good intentions; they won't accept responsibility when hurting others. Funny enough, there is money in making the future better, to invest in the changes that have to come—no matter how we now feel about them. Money is not bad; negative attitudes are. I have no wish to hurt anyone; if I do, I will try to explain and listen—try to make it better. Even so, I will not lie regarding how I feel." Of course, he didn't always tell people this; some already thought he was arrogant and would not comprehend what he meant. He could easily paint a picture in his head of where he allocated his resources. Sometimes his prediction could be off, but he made up for the losses each time he succeeded. Even so, these days, there was a feeling that kept hunting him, he tried to bury it, but it kept coming back. His feeling of time running out, his inability to buy himself the time he wanted. Even if there was a statistical probability that he would live many years to come, he could never know how many. For each day, there was one less to come; for each day, the next passed by faster than the previous one.

Before them, the city lights entered again. She saw a cab and signaled for it to stop. He opened the door for her as she gave him a shrewd look.
"It is true what you said, but isn't it also possible since you have the knowledge to make money, right? Imagine if you didn't have the money, everyone would only think you're a mad man doing what you feel like, wouldn't they?" She smirked, already knowing the answer.

2. OUR HISTORY

Bullying.
Trying to make me
look small.
You say it is my fault.

Maybe it is
what you think,
what it really is:
your inability
to live up to my potential.

Your envy
seeing me
exploring mine.

During the struggling years, he tried many things. When he was younger, alcohol or drugs; as he got older, meditation or working out to reduce or control the senses—constantly feeding him with an abundance of information. To feel calm, even if it was just for a moment. When spending time with her, he would feel the soothing feeling—feeling safe. Voices in his head would make sense. The moon had passed through the lunar phases since their rainy walk leaving the restaurant. As life went on, they longed for the brisk air and night sky that had captured them that night. Playfully one clear night, they decided to spend stargazing in a meadow.

When he lay his head on her chest, he felt drawn to her in a way that he couldn't get himself to move. With her, he could perceive the harmonic place which he previously only visited in his mind. As he lay there, he thought about how much she loved to read and study, *so curious about the essence of things*. It was seldom dull to talk to her. She spoke about the world, wondering about everything from the beginning of time, the development of life, the meaning of life, and what will come at the end of time. It had a calming effect on him. To have his existence understood in the context of the human race and its progress made him feel less important. Some might have thought it would not be a good thing to feel less important.

For him, it was exhausting with the constant feeling of being needed everywhere—by everyone. It combined with the frustration coming from his lack of understanding of why so many people seemed unable to think and make reasonable decisions for themselves. She made it all feel understandable; she could go on talking forever. He felt caught in her beauty when she did. As they spoke, he felt drawn into the center of our galaxy. In the journey towards singularity, all else was gone except for them. The size of the black hole allowed them to exist there, but they did not know what they would find around them during the experience—time had stopped. All their focus was on each other's minds. It was a pleasant feeling; to share so much information with someone listening, able to understand, who reflected with a willingness to explore—an experience unlike any he had with someone before. When talking to her, he felt so free. Finally, he felt heard for who he was and could also better hear himself. Even his deepest feelings, those he had kept since he was a child, could be felt. Even so, some thoughts dared not to share yet. Some shame and guilt had been on his mind for a long time. They lay quietly thinking with the sky above them, the force of gravity holding down their bodies. Their minds were free to wander wherever they wanted.

His relationship with her didn't feel real, not in a way that it would be any bad intentions; it just didn't feel like it could be for real. The way she acted felt unrealistic; she was a person he'd longed for in his imagination. When they spent time together, she would not ask anything else from him. He leaned towards her and kissed her to stop his thoughts for a while; it had a stimulating effect. As he sat himself up in the grass, she rested her head on his knee, tucking herself in with a wool blanket. She felt his hand gently stroking her hair. He felt secure in her presence, but somewhere inside, a voice told him not to believe it. It was all because of his crush; he could not see clearly.

Still, there was so much they didn't know about each other; he could not figure her out in the way he would with most people; he felt no need to figure her out— as if she was genuine. He had always figured everyone out, even when he didn't know that he knew —everyone's desire. Young and naive, he thought they meant what they said even when their bodies said otherwise. When he was young, this could often get him into trouble. He soon learned that people didn't want to know; they didn't want to know what they desired or why they acted as they did. He thought the whole society was walking around in a bubble; *everyone was so afraid of reality*. They could not handle it, so they were desperate to believe their lies. People lie all the time to each other, often because they care for each other. They do not want the other person to feel bad; they do not tell you how they feel because they want to be polite—not forcing you out of your emotional balance. It would hurt him how they wanted him to feel like interacting the same way as them; since he never felt like they did, how could he? He became differently treated for not responding as they did, set aside for not feeling like behaving in the way they thought was right. Only a kid, he didn't know that it was to become expected from him; he never felt like them, and no one asked him how he felt—only told him. *People told me that I am hard to deal with; well yeah, I get them because that is how I felt—about everyone*, he thought to himself. All was left for him to figure out by himself, with his voice speaking at a higher register, his heart pounding fast, his eyes always on the watch—frightened. He would talk fast even though he knew they wouldn't listen; even so, sometimes things had to be said.

People faked so much. He presumed it was another way to feel good about themselves; *maybe that was why they couldn't stand it when I told them the truth.* They made up stories to fit their emotions, to feel good about a situation. He would often see through their lies. Unknowingly and unwillingly, he learned to observe the meaning of their facial expression, leading to him knowing before they knew themselves. Since they didn't want to know—they didn't like him when he told them. He wanted to and also tried to make them understand what he saw, but they never did. His ability to learn what they wanted had him to be able to sometimes take advantage of them, and why shouldn't he use them from time to time? He knew it was wrong but could help himself from thinking; *it's not like they ever understood it.* Everything they did, he could do better if he just learned it; by acquiring the basic foundations and observing the structures. Even so, they tried to make him feel as though it was he who was stupid, stupid for not wanting to play their game—their emotional game of violence.

During his childhood, everyone had tried to push him to be something or do something; when he got the chance, he left and pushed them all away—it was all too painful to think of. He stood himself up, not wanting these memories haunting him now. She got up and placed herself by his side for a while. He hummed as a way of showing her he was not yet ready to talk; his brain felt worn out. He just wanted to be with her and experience the soothing feeling of her presence. Later, without speaking a word, they returned and rested on the ground again.

As they lay on the cold ground, eyes caught looking at the night sky; he told her about some of the violence he suffered through. The ruthless interactions he was a part of. She listened to him without uttering a word; he felt her fingers gently stroking his hand. When it got too intense to continue speaking, he left the cold ground sitting up. Moving up from the cold ground had him recall all the times he'd gotten up after a fight. He remembered the aching pain in his body, blood running down his nose, and all of his body was hurting—a cutting pain. He would feel contempt and ridicule but also relief; the moment of pain was finally over. It would never come again, other painful moments would, but this one had finally ended. The feeling of relief would be there regardless of whether he considered having won the fight or not; he was just glad that the moment had ended. Now curled up under the starlit sky, with his view on a glade, he could glimpse the treetops—slowly waving black against the dark sky.

Feeling the cold air through his nose gave him a brisk feeling as he continued:

"It always felt so meaningless; they would get back at me even harder if I were to fight back. If I didn't retaliate, they would maybe ease down for a while, but soon they would be back hurting me. I also tried to scare them, but there was no way to make it stop, not only the physical violence but also mental teasing and mind games—despicable things. No one ever made it stop, even if they knew what was happening. I was just a kid. No one ever gave me an alternative to play their game; I had to participate. In my mind, I knew there had to be other ways." She heard his voice shiver as he told her. She replied with a sympathetic voice:

"Yeah, even as a kid, you knew that violence was a waste of time; you were smarter than them. It was all about acting out their emotions at the moment for them; they couldn't think further ahead of the situation the way you do. I guess it was not what they said and did to you that was the worst part; as you said, sometimes what the community doesn't say or do pains you the most. The feeling that they know what is going on but never makes any real effort to make it stop. Each time that happens, they make you feel it was your fault, even if you know it is not. Why else wasn't anybody doing anything to change it? Why is it that they let us suffer? How could they just close their eyes?" He heard a trace of bitterness and strain in her voice. "They all blend into one person by creating a common perspective; all those people who told you that they would take care of you, protect you —who never did. Even worse, those who pretend like they cared but left you all the same. Their hypocritical joy and hopefulness felt only like a taunt. How could you ever put your faith in them when the system of their attempts was a constant failure? Could they not comprehend it themselves? How could you not blame yourself as no one seemed able to help? Them asking you to tell them how you feel, to open up, and for what? Judging. They never did anything. You have to go through the process of sharing your feelings; no one was listening—or understanding. The next time you don't want to talk about it; because they didn't do anything about it—then it's your fault. They argued that they couldn't help you because you won't talk to them. Well, they didn't help the other times, so why now should you put your faith in them? When I was young, they taught me to shut up; I learned how to listen until I finally could leave their judgment behind me." The loneliness haunted her the most as she grew up, always wondering; *why couldn't anybody just listen?* Even though she now knew why. Their eyes meet for just a moment before she continued:

"People can try to understand, but when showing compassion takes too much mental energy, they will start to moralize. After a certain amount of time, which depends on the person's understanding and ability to process information, you should have solved this problem yourself with the help they're offering. Otherwise, you are to blame. They won't admit that they don't get it; they are so used to having their perspective confirmed by others—they don't question it. They don't know how it feels to have no one to rely upon; according to their perception—they have done everything right. There could be nothing more to expect from them. The more complex the problem, or problems, the more you will have to bear the burden alone. You had to learn to take care of your well-being without being dependent on anyone else to have given it to you. According to contract law, it is to become considered a contract if two parties act recurrently; seemingly agree to the contract—even unspoken. When suffering through all the violence with no one interfering, they agree on it. It's part of the social contract. For a longer amount of time, you cannot change your painful situation; people will act like it is your fault. Acting as if you actually are that annoying; you don't try hard enough—deserving to be treated like that. In the end, you are alone. It is easier to blame yourself as well; at least then you have some sort of control, at least you can adjust your own behavior." He recognized himself in what she told him; this was a standard treatment for him growing up. It was rare that someone would genuinely acknowledge the horror they put him through. Instead, they usually ended up blaming his behavior and what he felt. As he felt her head on his shoulder, the acts still sounded unsavory when he talked about them. Even so, they were easier to tell.

The conversation awoke memories and feelings of a little girl. The trees in front of them made her remember how it felt to experience the forest, something she had done almost every day as a child— a girl who never really belonged. She remembered how many times she would try to explain, trying to get someone to help her, but they never understood. Never did anything that would really change things; explaining to her or others what was happening or making the abusers take responsibility. Helping her to leave and be able to evolve. Instead, she became torn down. When they told everyone to be friendly, for her to back down, all she could think was; *yeah, like that's going to help.* She knew how to be nice, but others did not. They had games in which they tried to force her not to be, twisting her words against her, not caring what she had to say. As they sat there, he felt her hand softly placed upon his; he told her something he had in mind for a long time:

"One of the most stressful things, an awful form of violence, is the part of not knowing, looks and feelings, communication through body language but unexplained by words. They are lurking, trying to get at you in some way. Passive aggressiveness, you know eyes are watching, you know that it is disdain towards you, but not in what way it will show itself. It could be yelling, disrespect, or physical violence; others not taking responsibility for their emotions make them unpredictably dangerous. At home, in relationships, or in school. It is like being watched by a predator, not knowing whether it will try and kill you or let you live. Yet the one targeting you pretends like they didn't do anything; they put you through all that stress and horror then pretends you are the one insane—imagining things. Everywhere I fucking went. I was scared all of my life, except for the moments alone in my head. In there, no one could hurt me. The drugs, everything, is a way to feel calm, to feel some joy for the lack of calmness I am able to feel with others. They only stressed me out. Judge me for being too clever or too harsh. They always tried to tell me how I felt and what was right. One of the saddest things is that they assumed I would be happy if I were just like them, that we were the same. They couldn't understand that for some people, their normal life will never be equal to happiness. Their way of lashing out their feelings made me feel like they were all kids; I had to calm them down—I guess they were." He thought about how he would often feel as if he had to dumb down everything he wanted to tell them, to break through the barrier of their emotional resistance towards what he had to say. "Did you know that when exposed to psychological violence, our brain reacts similarly as when exposed to physical violence?" She nodded. "The abuser knows they are in control by refusing to admit or take responsibility for their feelings and actions, leaving you with a stressful feeling. As long as they refuse to communicate, you don't know what danger to expect. It becomes hard to leave because of what might happen; they have control over you.". As he spoke, he remembered how liberating he felt the first time living alone, not fully understanding why at that point. "For some people, this behavior follows their whole life; keeping someone calm, never being able to leave because of the violence they would suffer. Their emotions are not being heard or understood. It is like they become used to holding themselves back, being under control, being the one left with all the blame. No one would understand because nothing is happening, right? But we are still animals; we still feel these things. The emotional programming and adjusting to violence make it so hard to leave. If you have no good relations, you only know how to react to the bad ones. You don't know how to react when treated well, so used to always being on your watch." He felt unburdened to say it aloud; he thought about how glad he was to have left that part of life behind— finally free. Finally able to make his own changes, not bound to their restrictions or limited by their imagination; a limitation he would later experience living with his previous wife as well. Sitting next to each other in the grass, tucked under the wool blanket, they looked into the night. Cold and dark like the memories they shared.

With a gentle touch, she lay her head on his shoulder, gazing upon his field of vision. They shared the experience as they relived different memories, sharing the pain. No word had she given him for a while, but he knew she had been listening as he'd spoken. He knew by glimpsing at her; her countenance showed that she had a profound focus, processing what he said—connecting the information. He felt an increased rhythm inside him; his heart was pounding faster as he continued with a low voice:
"I always wished to find a way to protect others from being hurt like that again, to find a way that keeps them from feeling alone and abandoned. I guess you know what I mean; I especially want to protect my

kids. My whole life, my family wondered why I never behaved as they did. Every time I tried expressing how I felt or what I had learned, their response would be to judge. To judge and criticize. For each time I decided to keep more and more to myself, I tried to explain in so many different ways, place, timing, all of it! Yet all they left me with was the stupid look on their faces or some unconsidered and hurtful comment." *Some things just make you feel like you are dying when thinking about it,* he thought before he continued:

"Even so, I am not someone who gives up; I made sure to beat them when playing the game they asked me to play. I got it all; family, house, education, job— better than anyone could imagine. Yet it still feels as if nobody shares any joy over my achievement, only some form of envying or, once again, stupid looks and faceless comments. It wasn't the words in the comments that hurt me; it was the lack of interest, the lack of knowing me—how hard I fought to get anywhere. It was all a surprise to them that I got this far; they lack the knowledge of all that I am capable of—waiting for me to fail. No one ever believed anything about me." Even when young, he knew he didn't belong with them. He felt betrayed while thinking; *no one around me even gave me the feeling that I might belong somewhere else.* He placed his elbow on his knees, his head sinking into his hands. All the anger he had felt for so long now seemed to come crawling back. "My family could not possibly think anything of me; it is still the case that they still never care enough to get to know me, to listen, no matter what I do. There is no longer anyone's opinion that I would actually care about, who could talk shitty about my actions. Those I care about know me; try to understand my intentions—help me when I am wrong."

Thinking about his childhood and family filled him with anger and guilt; the thoughts had been eating him up for a long time; he wished he would feel differently. As a kid, he really tried to love his family, but it only left him being taken advantage of; *fucking cunts*, he thought to himself. He would often swear in his head; luckily, few of the words ever left his mouth amongst others—only amongst those who knew him. From time to time, he thought his family had felt love for him; yet it could never stay that way—not if he acted like himself. That was not the kind of love he longed for. After all these years, he had come to terms with the fact that their relationship was this way; he could not expect more from them. His can-do spirit and grit had kept him striving all these years, especially when he knew he was right. Each person who gave him a piece of understanding would enhance his spirit. He searched for inducement in every way he could to keep on, no matter how hard things used to be. The more he learned, the more he became a better person through education, friends, colleges, and most of all—his kids. They made him see himself, both good and bad, understanding his behavior by thinking about how they saw him. Having them in his life urged his will to create a better future.

She had been sitting silent and still beside him, listening and thinking about what he said, recognizing her own devastation in his words. Both of them had been quiet for a while; she had now gathered her thoughts:

"I know that you wish that the abusers could understand what they have done to you, the pain you were put through. Somehow, you might think it would make you feel better; they suffer from knowing how much they've hurt you. That is why people try to hurt others back the same way they were hurt; instead, using empathy takes a lot of cognitive thinking. To understand what others are going through, not jump to the conclusion that someone only wishes to hurt you. It is also a mindset of wanting to extend your perspective from your own. Would you expect a predator to feel bad for the victim as it kills it? No. Why? Because of its limited cognitive functions, it simply can't think of a way to find a way to get what it needs without harming others. Unable to understand the effect it causes, it uses violence to take control for its survival. It can't communicate with others as we do, it feels as if it is the right thing to do, and it is since it has to in order to survive. People do the same thing, just acting out their emotions. You must let go of the anger towards them, the anger over how they treated you. Instead, you may see them only as animals. Then you will see them neutrally as objects part of this world; in essence, beings wishing you no harm but who are too affected by emotions. Some humans cannot understand others' perspectives by using rational thinking—unable to communicate." She had to figure out ways to understand the iniquity she saw in the world; some would consider her understanding a brutal form of thinking—he understood how it was also true. She continued speaking with a neutral tone in her voice:

"From what you told me, you've been exposed to violence. No matter what you say, how you now feel, or what you have become—they still wounded you when you were young. It left you with a damaged coding to your way of thinking about yourself and cooperating with others. Always have been on your watch trying to prevent more violence; without understanding it yourself—all because of how you became treated. You longed to feel control since you never had love" he felt distressed as she mentioned his longing for control "I can see that you now seem to have learned a new way, reprogramed your brain by understanding a better way of thinking. Still, the violence is a part of you, an experience that you cannot remove nor forget what it felt like. It is a part of your physical memory, sometimes uncontrollable when you react in relation with other people." What she said was true; he sometimes found himself holding back impulses to say things and think thoughts connected to his previous experiences— trying to protect himself in different ways. Their voices now sounded louder, more lively, and he replied:

"It is true, and you know that humans under stress tend only to remember the angry faces they see. We seek potential threats and interpret the world as perilous when exposed to stress. I guess we who have become exposed to stress for so long keep that feeling with us easily triggered. Fear makes you experience as if you are entering a different world, a world you cannot escape, a world full of violence in which you must protect yourself. I guess it is connected to our instinct to withdraw while exposed to stress; when we live with stress for too long, we are to protect ourselves by avoiding contact with others. When we feel calm, we feel free to explore the world because we feel like we have the energy to survive a potential downfall." She knew this was true, thinking about all those times when she was young, feeling paralyzed by her fear, preventing her from doing things she longed for—following her desires.

"Yes, and also that we have people who help us if exposed to danger or being hurt. Without the feeling of protection from others, it is hard to dare", she said as his words recalled all those times she felt haunted by looks and actions, how her fear had her self-centered as if everyone was out to get her. Every day she'd try to make sure to remind herself and her kids that it is not the case, that most people will care for them, and that arguments are happening regardless of their actions. Reminding them that all is well, reminding them how much she loved them, the love that keeps the judging voices at ease. Enhance the esteem of their goodness and sufficiency. His eyes showed signs of a defeatist mood. Still sitting next to him, she rested her head on his shoulder. Her voice now turned into softly speaking:

"Normally nowadays, more people get to grow up in peace, less become neglected, at least here. Those who get hurt may still suffer, but many have parents who support them and make them feel safe. You had none of that, just yourself; no wonder you have trouble trusting others. You became limited by the perception of the world by those around you, by their animalistic behavior. It is also why they treated you as they did; it was impossible for them to understand your feelings based on the threats you experienced. Therefore they judged and punished your behavior instead of understanding it." She found comfort in reading about the safety and joy others would perceive in their life, unable to change her own.

They noticed something moving in the glade, almost impossible to hear; she found herself drawn even closer to him as he laid his arm around her. Usually, she felt distressed being near someone except for her kids; with him, her oxytocin level would run high, connecting to him, almost like a drug—it had her feel safe to speak. She noticed his voice having a higher register, sounding forced, as he replied:
"It is hard to think about what they did to us; they took away something almost as important as oxygen for our bodies. That is how important relationships are; without others—we fucking die. They had us

beaten and stressed out, so we had an even harder time connecting with others, all for their amusement and lack of self-control. They made us look bad because they couldn't understand us, extending their perspective to others through spiteful words. We survived, but they made us struggle for survival. No wonder some of us died; loneliness, not being understood and safe, is a deadly disease. Yet those who infected us are bullies; they laugh at others' pain and suicide—so used to violence and its culture. Incapable of visualizing another type of connection built on love and trust. Masking their intellectual insecurity with violence; unable to gain influence using language and sharing knowledge. Not able to keep others calm, only stressing others out; not able to show compassion instead only judging and ridiculing—controlling others." Many faces came to mind, people he had met during the years; they filled him with reluctance. She sat straight and responded with a faceless expression; her eyes lost looking into the forest:

"You are right, but there is no use in blaming them; they could not change their behavior any more than we could. That's just it! They didn't have the knowledge or the cognitive thinking—mere animals. Violence becomes deeply embedded in many childhoods, seemingly to find no alternative way to act; we all make the best of what we get—those who wanted to help you did want to but couldn't find any way. Finally, we are able to leave most of them who hurt us behind, let them and their way of living be dead to us now. You have lived amongst the darkest of human existence. In time, this behavior will be consumed by the new world since they cannot comprehend all the complicated structures that build this world; in time, they will lose power. The more I got rid of people who judged, the more I became free to live my life as I wanted; explore the boundaries of my imagination. Nowadays, it is possible to bring my own meaning to my existence. I never want to lose hope; I either try to change something—if I am unable to, I will do my best to accept what was and is. It is important to talk about what was, but I will not dwell on my thoughts of how things should have been; or how I wanted them to be. I won't dwell because none of that matters now; I will not know, and I cannot know. People tend to decide others' futures based on their past, but we are all in power to make new choices; suppose we allow ourselves to learn from our past knowledge—allow ourselves and others to be good. By helping us understand, we free ourselves from our differences and can keep trying to connect with others." She had been caught in her

misery during times, trying to figure it all out. He replied, giving her a thoughtful look:
"I guess you're right, but what does it mean for us? That we can't expect more from them? Everyone always does their best in every situation, even though some act awful and without regret. We all are beings, limited by the preconditions we were born and grew up with, all leading to a given situation. No human can possibly understand all of it. Are we all to only try and respect each other's decisions? And take responsibility for our own then, I guess." These thoughts had also occurred to him before but never connected in this context.

She responded with determination in both her eyes and voice:
"Humans will always hurt each other; we are different, and therefore, it brings misunderstandings when we communicate. They sat us aside when young because we differ from them; moralizing different behavior was necessary in order to keep humans together as a group. They need to have a shared understanding of good behavior to feel good and appear eminent to themselves. We are obligated to find knowledge and new ways of communicating, helping us better understand each other. For those who refuse to, or more likely are unable to understand

or accept responsibility, we have to try and neutrally identify and understand why an act is violent—identifying what effect it had on the other person. Try to prevent them from hurting others when connecting; we must find ways to keep us all connected. We don't have the cognitive resources to fully understand history and foresee the future; prevent us from being hurt again. We can only learn what's important, makes us feel good, and focus on increasing that part of our lives. In human evolution, the psychopath's behavior, lacking empathy, was beneficial; it would allow some to act violently and thereby protect the group from outsider danger and horror. Instead of judging people's behavior, we should understand the intentions behind their actions. What is their intent when doing what they do? What is it that led them to do it? How do they function?" It had been hard for her to accept this conclusion. His face showed signs of skepticism as she continued, "as you know, there is no way to make them stop by trying to scare them or retaliate; only by knowledge. It's true for all conflicts; the only way to reduce violence in the world—ending wars. Violence only brings more violence. Only by understanding what is happening and taking responsibility can we make it better, not by dwelling in the past on what should have been or asking people to be what they are incapable of being. If they are unable to understand, we must understand them as the animals they are; find ways to prevent them from hurting others. It also means we must take responsibility and forgive ourselves for all our mistakes on our way to becoming better people. We all do our best." It was a liberating thought to let go of all the horror, leaving it to the past and letting all of their new memories take their place.

A bright red light in the sky told them that morning had broken, the blankets had kept them heated, but they longed for the warm comfort of the indoors; he stood up and gave her a hand to help her rise. With a tired look and with a humble smile upon his face, he spoke:
"Let us leave these memories here and find our way home" she nodded and took his hand. Both of them were too tired to speak another word.

Hearing it all aloud broke his heart, but it also had an apprehensiveness like everything else. He could better understand his feelings. At some point, it no longer felt as painful or hard to deal with; it was just something he had been through a long time ago, something that once had happened—a story long ago told and long ago forgotten.

3. OUR CONSCIOUSNESS

The knowledge of the time;
always a clock, a calendar.
Makes us think we can plan our lives,
believing we have to.

But living is not planned;
life is moments,
moments of feelings.
You can never make a plan
for what you will feel.

You can never plan a happy future.
Only look for joy in every moment
and take care of people.
People who make you feel loved.

Time. Measuring the earth rotating on its axis and how it is revolving around the sun. Using mathematics to understand the world and predict future events. *She often found herself thinking about how she could have expressed more of her love during their time together; could she possibly have prevented her friend from experiencing the loneliness leading her friend to leave this existence?* Time is in the perception of distance between events when moving in spacetime. Still, time can also show itself through programming in our bodies in which order events will occur; our biological clock. Experiencing time depends on our focus and how much attention we pay to it. Our perception of time is a product of the amount of time compared to the years we have lived. *When she remembered the scent of her friend, her eyes started to tear.* As it is with money, we are born into this world, never knowing how much time we'll have. Time and money are two humanly created concepts used as a way to measure reality and collegiate humanity. *Ten years had passed since she lost her friend.* The way time is measured is much different from how it is perceived.

T hey continued sharing their lives and experiences. In a way, he had gotten used to having her by his side conversing about all and nothing. Her joking and laughing was an everyday phenomenon that he couldn't picture himself living without. Sometimes she felt as if they were children teasing and playing. She once told him:
"Some admonish me that I act like a child; well, hell yeah, I do. Children are innovative and exploring. If

being a grown-up is just about following everyone else's rules and doing things you have to: what's the point? Then I might as well be replaced by a machine." She was almost always kind of joking—it made reality feel a little easier. Her friends would appreciate it, but no one except him ever made her feel easier in the same way. He would find new ways to amuse her; the joke would often contain a brutal statement of the reality we live in. Humor is a way to capture and describe feelings; describe something hard in a simple matter. Playing with misunderstandings that happen as we try communicating. As well as she did, he could also easily explain things vividly and beautifully, like only the brightest amongst them she knew could. He was so calm yet still playfully curious and enthusiastic. She loved how he always seemed eager to learn more.

It had become recurrent that he found himself waking up by her side, but he had trouble sleeping this night. His mind would give him no peace until he figured out a solution. The sound of his footsteps left a silent echo as he wandered around in his bedroom. He observed the lights and movement on the streets below. Stars were lost in the city lights, much unlike the sky they observed lying in the meadow. He felt as lost in the city as the stars seemed to be. Only in nature could he now be found. As she woke up, she first watched him in silence before gently delivering her observation:

"It looks like you feel a lot of anxiety; maybe you need to share your thoughts?" Her eyes were now focused on the roof above her but still catching a glimpse of his movements. He turned towards her but then kept walking around again as he replied:

"With whom? Who could understand and give me any rational thoughts about it? Who would take the time? And even if they do; no one dares to tell me the truth. Every advice anyone ever gives, I have already thought about; I am so sick of people telling me stuff I already know. No one knows the company as I do; no one knows my life aspirations as I do—well, that would be you. Others only focus on one thing; it is always the current business—unable to comprehend my vision. I have rearranged the whole structure at work; no one even cares—they only complain. It works better now, but it is no use to tell them; they don't think about it or wish to understand it." *They didn't understand the previous structure either,* he thought to himself. His feeling of desolation had his voice sound harsh, but he was not mad at her. He was not angry with his colleagues either. Those closest to him would always try to give him helpful advice about his life and the business; they did care a lot for each other. He didn't think they were useless; he depended on their knowledge, but they often had difficulty understanding how his brain processed information. During the years, the practice had made him better at providing a short and concrete explanation—a way they would easier understand. When needing advice in complex situations, he would often carefully choose whom to ask to be sure to get a well-reasoned answer. He would find wisdom in what others said; for each well-reasoned piece of advice, he would try to paint himself a picture. It enabled him to store it in his mind and use it when he connected information. He would get a frustrating feeling when people were afraid to take action; at times when he presented a solution that some people would seem to be against without offering a reasonable alternative. He would get mad when they would not accept logical deduction, forcing him to go against it— hiding behind excuses and prejudice.

He always tried to give all employees what they needed, wanting them to succeed and enjoy sharing his ambition. He had a hard time accepting those who refused to change, refusing to evolve because it was hard for them. Using their energy fighting against changes instead of trying to understand. *Protecting themselves from admitting their inability to adapt to new ideas,* they had him thinking. He felt how the frustration came from the struggle in his head, trying to comprehend what to do, how to change a stagnant situation. He longed for a logical solution to make it all better.

She sat herself up in bed with eyes looking at him. He held his hands clasped over his head. She saw his back as he stood on the other side of the room. A reflection in the window showed a blurry image with signs of his dispirited visage. As she used to see him with coworkers at work or at other gatherings, she was amazed at his kindness and patience with others. He would often be quiet, listening, in order to find ways of helping them. He gave them thoughtful reflections about the situation; his form of caring, even if sometimes he told them things they were not ready to hear. She appreciated that he would always try and listen to them. Without being affected by his frustration, she replied with a calm voice:

"Well, maybe they don't know you—most people won't. Most people don't listen, but I want to. Most people can't mentally process all information as they listen or talk; they need more time. Maybe others are unable to understand the business, your visions, but most of all—you. You are a complex man. Others will not tell you the truth as you see it. Maybe they don't care enough about you to tell you the truth or can't handle talking about it. Other people have helped you before by contributing the information from which you have learned; through the stories shared in books and movies—you do benefit from others. Even if I don't get it, an open mind to talk to can ease a troubled mind; it helps to say these things out loud to someone willing to listen." Her voice indicated that she tried to accompany him; her reasoning brought him an assuaging feeling to his anxiety.

"Well, I would like to take the time to talk to you about it, but these days I am at the office a hundred hours a week. Between that and spending time with my kids, I don't know if I could get the time." In the end, she heard how his voice softened with a sigh. Without looking at her, he sat against the windowsill, his head resting in his hands.
"You can't spend one of our nights talking about this with me? Do you have to work a hundred hours a week? This is not the priority you once told me you have; that you do as you feel like. If so, how could you tell me that you are free? Free to choose what to think about? I am just wondering. To be happy, you have to be able to do things for your interest and amusement—to feel like it. But maybe you have been

controlling your feelings for too long. Well, of course, you did; because you could. Since you felt lonely, you didn't care whether they liked you or not." He was taken aback by the sudden cogent in her voice. "You used your competence and swayed them, had them admire your success, but the feeling of loneliness doesn't go away now, does it? You still feel the same as when they despised you—don't you? It doesn't matter if they admire or despise you; you still aren't one amongst them. You wish not to be envied but to be seen for who you are. You are good with numbers, aren't you? Counting, controlling your time and money. You can make it as efficient as you please. This pleases you, but you cannot count or control your feelings in this matter; it is harder. You cannot order them nor find solutions for them by yourself. They have to take their time, time which you wish to control. You can change the way people think about you by acting the way they want you to, but this takes too much of your energy; to constantly think about your behavior and the stress caused by the uncertain outcome of their feelings. I know it is intriguing with things that can be measured; that follow structures and patterns rather than the complicated mess feelings are."

She felt how he gave her a sharp look as she continued: "you became a master of information in order not to need others in the same way. It is not because of the lack of wanting to share your thoughts and feelings, rather than wanting to share them with someone who can understand you for who you are— not for who you know how to be. Sometimes it is easier to live solving problems in the future; when it is too hard to connect with people and the feelings you are having in the present. Let go of those around you who only wish for something from you. You have been stressed for so long; your mind needs peace, a break from this existence and all surrounding you. Let us travel somewhere and find some serenity for a while; find emotional comfort. I believe only in that way it might become clear to you what you must do." She had a certain eagerness to her voice, but her body language remained calm. He found no arguments regarding her reflection on his behavior. It felt liberating to hear her say it. To become heard, to become understood.

"I have all these deadlines coming up. I can't take a vacation; how could that help?" His voice indicated he had been listening but was not yet convinced. He let his hands down and turned his head, looking at her.

"As I said, if you don't, you can't have your mind be free to think of the solutions you need to achieve it. I know you hate to repeat information, but the information runs loops in your brain. Sometimes you have to hear things a hundred times to fully understand what it means, to structure and process the information in a different but safe and silent environment; by repeating information, we learn to foresee what will happen." He could feel her determination through the sound of her voice.

"I appreciate how you are just so annoying. Most people are just boring; you annoy the shit outta me with your reasoning," she could see his grin and the fondness in his eyes as he said it, "it is always nice to get some insightful advice." There was a long-term silence. They then heard the coffee maker's switch turn off in the kitchen.

Silently sitting at the kitchen table with their first cup of coffee, she observed the cause of entropy, chaos increasing as the oat drink entered the black coffee. Heat even out until finding a new solid state at room temperature. She was caught in her thoughts, her working understanding, about what the universe will be like when reaching maximum entropy. She shared some thoughts with him:

"You know the world around us is built up by different mathematical structures, organized in different ways leading to particles being created, floating, fluctuating, almost like dancing around in fields. Everything is always moving. Elementary particles, electrons, and quarks make atoms and matter; this is the current understanding of the coding that creates the universe in which we live. That creates preconditions for life itself—the precondition for our bodies and minds. Our social groups have programmed our minds to register and perceive the world in a certain way. A way that would allow us to collaborate with other human beings in the effort to achieve the great quest; to evolve and save life itself from destruction. To do so, we must make it better for the next generation. It is not strange that we feel so deeply for our children; that has to be the case so that we fulfill the endeavor that is to survive. All in order to survive and save the children. It is also not strange that we have the strong need to try and make things better, more efficient; it is built in the code of human DNA." He looked at her, wondering where her thoughts would take them this time. Intrigued, his eyes followed her as she continued:

"Imaginativeness is a powerful trait; for those with great imagination, it is important to keep the balance between the universe as it is perceived by the great mass and how they perceive it. Otherwise, they might end up losing connection with the group—losing the ability to communicate with other humans. At times when ambitions become too far from reality that society can perceive, it is still important to connect with others. That is why we are so dependent on whom we have around us, whom we have by our side. Madness can be how one is perceived by others; if they can not simply understand you, you might be considered strange or mad—leading you to associate yourself in such a manner. If just someone understands, that could be all that saves you from losing your mind. Some of us lose our minds in loneliness. I have known that loneliness; for a long time, my mind longed to connect with someone who could understand." Her eyes left sight of the coffee mug in which the oat drink was now fully merged with the coffee. She was grateful for the friends she now had. When she got to know them, she would start to feel accepted without holding back too much of herself. With them, she could grow, and even if they didn't fully understand her, they would still accept her. She could not fully understand them either, but they would still care as much for each other. He smirked and replied while standing up, walking to the kitchen counter to pour himself another cup of coffee:

"Oh dear, you sound like such a wacko, but it makes sense when you put it like that."

"I know, right? I don't think that you are a mad man, not yet, but you have the potential to be." She said, smiling at him, "some of us have great potential, but we are also affected by what and whom we have around us. Also, whether we are able to let people in or not." The way she had said it was with so much care and love. *Not that others might get it*, he thought to himself, but he knew her. She had observed during their time together how much he tended to hold back, even amongst friends, seemingly daring in his statements. He would often keep them at a distance; she knew there was a part of him they didn't know. She knew how hard it had been for her to start trusting people, to dare expect something of them, but also how much it had strengthened their relationship when she did. Even so, she knew he held back because she still did as well; she had observed their pattern. His voice sounded amused as he replied:

"Well, when they tell you about me; that I was fucking mad—they are right." She heard the playfulness in his voice. She replied to his statement smirking and with rolling eyes. He placed the coffee mug on the kitchen table and positioned himself behind the chair she was sitting on, laying his arms around her. He could not resist nudging his nose in her hair to seize the scent that would sometimes make him feel nearly sedated. He thought about what she had tried to tell him; *there is a difference between being accepted and being understood.* To become appreciated for your good deeds or to become understood for the intentions behind your actions.

She let her head rest against his arm, thinking about how much she valued his presence. She then spoke:
"If once we've felt lonely and excluded, our instinct tells us to find a way to never experience that again. That instinct is the reason many hang on, trying to make it work in an unhealthy relationship. Even if it is not true that we physically seem to be lonely, we need those who understand and know us for who we are. By staying in a relationship where you are not appreciated for who you are, in which you are not understood, you will probably feel even more lonely. When feeling lonely and depressed, we experience other people as a potential threat and therefore have a harder time connecting with others. Even though some might say they make it on their own, it is not entirely true. They still need to feel as if they have people they can rely on if needed; we need to have others who help us but also to feel needed—to be of

use to others. All to keep sane. Even so, I wish not to marry again."

"No, not me either." he softly snorted as he said it, still standing behind her and keeping his arms around her. She continued with a cheerful voice:

"Though I would like to know all you know if you are willing to share with me. I guess it would have us spending a lifetime together."

"Always learning from each other," he smiled.

"Always learning more," she replied, looking up at him, returning the smile.

"You have such strong opinions about everything, don't you? The world won't stand a chance as you figure it out", he said, sniggering as he lifted her hair and kissed her neck.

"Yeah, quite tedious, don't you think?" She said with sarcasm and sighted from enjoying his approach, twisting her head to reveal her neck, longing for his kisses to continue.

"Never." He said and let his kisses follow her lead.

"Well, you know, never say never!" She playfully replied. Then there was no talking. Experiencing each other's presence only with their bodies.

Later they sat down to finish the now at room temperature second cup of coffee, feeling relaxed but still caught by the clock informing them about the need to soon break the moment to leave for work. Noticing the clock had her feeling frustrated, she shared her thoughts:

"We have more things, food, and better health care than we could have wished for a hundred years ago, but more people feel lonely. Humans are not meant to operate on a scale of this many relationships we go through in life to withhold the system. With everyone selling their time working or trying to get a job, less and less have time for caring for each other whenever they feel like it. Always ruled by a clock aggravates us from caring by little gestures that say you include one another, actions that make us feel like a part of a community. We now buy services instead of genuinely helping each other out. I guess this is why many feel as if they have no one to rely on; their relationships become hollow as they try to keep their life together. It is hard for humans to live in this new world, adjusting our feelings to time frames. We are meant to cooperate in smaller groups through life, not in this plenitude of different communities over time. We lose track of the people around us; we lose track of ourselves. There are things we can't know about ourselves; therefore, we need others to tell us. People close to us who will care and understand; tell us even when we don't want to hear it but need to hear it in order to move on." His eyes started to focus on the clock ticking on the kitchen wall as he processed what she'd just said.

His field of view wandered; he was caught by her reflection in the window, how beautiful her contour looked. It gave him the feeling as if he saw them in a movie. Even if he never would have wanted to stay amongst the same group he grew up in, the struggle to keep up with everyone around him was challenging. People would change their jobs at work, neighbors moved, and he moved. His kids had different friends during preschool and school; it was hard trying to keep up with their relationships as well. Even if he would connect with some, they might soon be gone. He had them who had been by his side for years and considered them close friends, but he thought about how they seldom could arrange for them to meet outside work; *there are always so many people coming together, so much to talk about*. He appreciated his conversations with her; they had room for silence and reflections—as well as engagement in their ideas. His engagement would be something that drove others away. Even so, he felt as if he had less time to spend with her as well. Keeping it all together —there was never enough time. As his thoughts wandered, he asked her:

"But why is it that when we feel lonely or misunderstood, we bring forth behavior that makes it harder to cooperate? Like pushing those around us, is it because we want to make ourselves feel safe? I used to push others by continue asking questions they were not ready to answer or hadn't figured out yet. I just felt the need to get an answer. When they did not respond as I wanted them to or seemed unable to understand me, I tended to feel even more lonely; the feeling just got worse." This was a common problem for him when he tried to present an idea or solution that others would not seem to get. He knew his colleagues and friends would get frustrated with him, sometimes thinking he did not care for their feelings —even though he was often right in the end. He would be considered cold and unempathetic, and they would get mad at him. In the end, they would often appreciate his ideas and come back to him to follow his lead; but he had to hear lots of shit before they got there. He could understand that they worked differently from him and, therefore, vice versa. Still, knowing that would never enable him to work the same way as them. On the occasions he was wrong, he'd be satisfied for being proved wrong, grateful for someone who had listened and shared their knowledge in a way for him to understand.

She looked at him, thinking about how his way of impatiently pursuing a goal was one of the things she liked most about him. She loved keeping up with his wild ideas and sudden changes, all of which followed an underlying structure she understood and appreciated. She knew the behavior of pushing others from her own experience as well—it affected both of their lives. She answered him with a compassionate voice:

"Pushing them causes frustration or stress, but you also do it because of the same, I guess. Sometimes you long for the feeling of control when you feel as if you can't put your trust in them—not understanding each other's perspectives. The trust between people builds on their emotional bond of accepting their needs for each other. It is hard to follow the logic behind it, but it is necessary for us in order to survive; humans are deeply entangled with each other. For most people, it takes time to adapt to new ideas, as you said, and most of the time, neither you nor they know how long. You can only tell them what you think or how you feel; then it is up to them— otherwise, they will feel forced to do it. Some changes have to be made; they must decide to follow your lead or leave, and you must listen when they communicate what they need. It is also important to see through what it is that you really can offer, to make it clear to yourself when you speak with those who do not understand you. When stressed, our body thinks we might get hurt or die; that we don't have time to think it through. It will force us to do what is necessary to survive: fight or flight. Functions in our brain that allow us to focus, reflect, analyze or be empathic are reduced; functions that help us understand others' perceptions of the situation. Even if it seems as if they don't care, many do—same as you. It is just especially hard for those under stress to understand; it is also the same for us. Trying to calm yourself and figure out what you are contributing to in a situation with others will make you aware of how you affect the situation—to understand when you are getting stressed. It will lead you towards better expressing your intentions to others, no matter whom you're talking to." She found her behavior sometimes had driven her to control people in a way she never intended; she wished for them to understand.

"Well yeah, that is true; the only behavior to try to control is my own," he said, finding himself to concur with her reflection.

"Yeah, you never want to hurt anyone, right? Not forcing them to do or feel as you like them to only for your own sake; you want them to know why. No intelligent being would choose violence, putting someone in distress if you could talk it through. You want them to be genuine. You do what you do to make your world better, yet you end up hurting them if they aren't emotionally ready to hear what you have to say. You want to be able to fail, feel as though you can be wrong but make up for it, to be able to learn without others judging your ideas before hearing them out. You want them to be curious about your ideas, but it is hard to find these people, even harder to create and withhold a connection. I used to spend my time focusing on what others did, trying to be like them. Now I spend time with those who accept me for who I am, then spend the rest of my time dreaming. I love the way it feels like time stops when I connect the information in my mind—or when talking to you about it. For me, everything feels magical until I learn it. I can usually master it if I learn it; when I understand its relevance, I can connect the information with everything else. I love connecting new ideas to new and old information, I don't know how many times my understanding has changed, but I am glad each time I figure something out. I think I understand the world, but then I learn something new, and my perception changes again." When she finished speaking, she was left looking at him with an irrepressible look.

His body was immersed on the chair, sitting across the table from her; he smiled, thinking about what she'd said.

"You are such an artistic mess, and you know how my brain works; I can't stop trying to understand messes that others think are impossible to understand. Okay, I actually don't think you are a mess. I think you are a reasonable human, no matter what apprehension others have of you. You are the most startling one I have ever met. It is amazing how you long for knowledge; most people are willing to pay others a lot to avoid extending theirs." She reservedly gazed at him, flattered by his comment. His anxiety had left him during their time together. The clock indicated that they were supposed to leave in order to be on time for work. 66186948744120 steady electromagnetic pulses had been counted from vibrating cesium-133 atoms.

4. OUR FUTURE

Never follow
someone using fear.
The promise of destruction.
Keeping you afraid,
keeping you in line.

Always follow
someone using compassion,
trying to understand.
Keeping you calm.
Your thoughts should be free.

Beauty lies within simplicity. *In his head, he heard a baby crying.* Understanding what is hard to grasp in a sensual way—an interpretation of the world we perceive with our emotions. In essence, life's all about statistics and probabilities. *The beauty lay in the existence of his baby, the odds that all events occurred so his baby had the ability to live, and the probability of the adorable person his daughter was and would become in his eyes.* Everything is connected, and all your actions are an inevitable part of the outcome of all you do. You affect everything, and yet all you are is statistics. *The face turned white as he lifted his baby from the cradle. Then there was no time, no place. Existence contained mere agony. He blamed himself for all he wished he had done differently, his part in the events in which he had not been able to prevent this outcome.*

· ·

T he acoustics awoke him; playing felt so long ago now. They sat on the old wooden floor that squeaked as they moved. His fingers wandered against the strings of an old acoustic guitar, trying to find harmony in the chords. With a look, he encouraged her to sing; he loved the sound of her voice. Experiencing music and playing together made him feel present; it made him feel placid, existing only in the concordance—an easy heart. During times of pressure or tragedy in his life, the harmony would disappear. It made him feel as if something had stolen the music from him, the music was playing, but it would feel meaningless to him. With her, he could finally hear it again; the exonerative feeling was there. None of them had ever created music on a stage, but both of them loved the beauty in the harmony it would bring. In life, he was often in-between feeling numb or exhilarated. At times he felt the numbness he still would feel but kept his emotion hidden. Painful feelings were changing into physical pain in his body. Pleasant feelings were enjoyable moments of life he had forever lost.

Softly singing next to him, she lay her head against his shoulder. Feelings of pain, loneliness, joy, and love came to life through the sound of her voice. Sounding as if she finally liberated all emotions she had kept to herself. At times it would pain him when he heard her speak; it became evident that she had been in conflicts before. Conflicts she couldn't resolve; disputes because of who she was, all that she loved. Her curiosity and humor, longing for an understanding, her longing to figure out love, her eagerness to figure out life. He admired how she seemed to be unable to hate anything thoroughly. Even if she understood his frustration when he described it, she always tried to understand what was behind, what led up to the situation, no matter how complex. He thought of a way to compliment her for that as he heard her singing voice fading, laying the guitar next to him.

"You have such tremendous strength, all you've been through, all the shit people put you through; still, you try to understand."

"Strong? I know the fuck not," she snorted, "but I have decided not to kill myself; in time, death will come anyway. I guess that keeps me motivated to keep exploring the world—search for meaning and be good." Her lips turned into a bitter smile, "but yeah, I am sorry if it sounds like I know what I am talking about; I have no fucking idea how to live, but this is my way of coping with it. I appreciate that you see me trying." In the end, she gave him a humble look. The rain was smattering on the windows and the plastic roof on the porch. The previous heat from the sun shining all morning seemed to have left the house. In the faraway cabin, there was not much more for them to do than be close to each other. Sitting next to each other on the floor, she shared her reasoning with him:

"Well, the world just is as it is, the matter we see and the matter of us; life created that has coded the matter in different ways for us to understand. Depending on the programmed understanding, language, our consciousness make us think of the world in a certain way. Since the world only exists, everything—every right or wrong view, is just different interpretations. If someone interprets the world in a certain way, it still is the true world for them. When changing groups and surroundings, I guess we might actually end up in different worlds in that sense. I am amazed each time my perception, my truth, changes. That is why it is so important for us to have faith and be empathic; if we aren't—the world won't be either." She thought about how the knowledge had inspired her to move on during hard times as she continued: "even if people do things that make us feel otherwise, we have to try; try to say yes and be intrigued by others' ideas—it's always about where your focus lies. Focusing on good or bad things decides the truth as you know it. The only way to keep this mindset is to understand what makes you feel otherwise. To remove yourself from all that makes you feel less than you are, to remove yourself from whom others decide you are. Leave the surroundings and find new people, good people who will see you for who you are and want to be like." Her words reminded him of what she had told him before; curious, he asked her:

"You keep talking about how we program our brains; you make it sound like we are computers." He had heard others speak in such matters before and was interested in hearing her take on it. Her eyes told him that she was keen to tell him as she replied:

"There is a code for everything; all you see can become described by mathematics. We all have the coding in our DNA. Humans are basically just entities changing information with each other, aren't we? We are all just a bunch of lonely entities longing to connect. All our sensations let us register information that affects an understanding of the world surrounding us; without a programmed understanding, the information is just there—without a preferred way of being observed. The world exists as it is, just like information stored on the computer's hardware; the information there could exist without the running software enabling us to perceive the information on a screen. The organization of information in different fields creates every particle, atoms that later formed our biological composition—this creates the world in which we live. The categorization and organization of information in our brain, perceived by our senses, later makes us understand the experience of the world in which we live. Like the organization of information in the computer. Does it makes sense to you?" She finished speaking, giving him a look of curiosity.

"Sure, I haven't thought about it quite like that before, but it is definitely an interesting perspective." Thinking about how changes were merely information rearranging, he recalled how the changes had been a crooked road for him. Somehow he seemed to have gotten used to the constant change, to push himself to rearrange the information he learned to new circumstances. He had to learn a lot and find new, good-minded people in order to make it possible. From how he saw others dealing with changes in life, he gave her a doubtful look and continued:

"It's hard to program a good mindset, having to go against a mad mob—the modern form of the angry peasants, you know," he said sarcastically, thinking about the line of reasoning in news articles, "the one that follows an emotionally driven cause or human. We see it all the time; someone starts a story and pushes everyone to believe it. The idea gives a fixed answer, and people long to believe it. The more people who follow the idea makes it even more prominent. Those who question it become regarded as mad by the mad mob; people who try using logic and adding all the pieces together." As he spoke, he recalled how he would try to argue with these people about seeing things from a neutral, broader perspective when he was younger; *why did it always have to be someone's fault?* "The mad mob always follows someone's feelings regarding seemingly right or unfair events in their eyes. Maybe the leader wants to succeed in gaining political power, fighting for the rich, fighting for the poor, saving the earth, having equal rights, or catching a criminal. It can be basically anything that a person wants to become seen in a certain light, even things that are logical in essence, but then they twist the cause for personal gain. It feels as if they try to hide reality by focusing on the emotional perspective; some argue there is no way to make a change without playing on people's emotions, playing with feelings—refusing to understand the other person's perspective. Someone or some others are soon to be convicted; the opposite group never speaks the truth. It might also be so that they don't, but it is also true that most people don't—and what is the truth? It can also be a failure to understand the other person's perspective leading both parties to see the other one as liars—but who is really the liar? Who is entitled to their perspective?" as he said it, he thought about how this had kept him puzzled during the years; to wonder who spoke the truth—*could I even apprehend it?* She gave him a neutral reply:

"Maybe it would be the most logical thing to stop speaking about the truth and just try to understand what physically happened; where we are now, as we talked about under the starlit sky. Since we only speak from our own perspective, isn't it always storytelling? We always use language created from our imagination to try and make up a story for what happened at that moment. We only remember what we paid attention to, where our focus lay at a given moment—the rest we make up in our minds. For each time we remember, we alter our memories. Using our imagination when describing things, the things we experienced. I sometimes wonder if the imagined stories are any different. All stories become based on information we have processed, based on our experiences; whether it's true depends on whether someone shares the perspective with us. Different stories about history—or what is appropriate behavior affect how we perceive the world throughout our lives. We all carry our own truth, unable to understand the world or others' perspectives fully. Instead of arguing over who did the right thing, perhaps we should hear both perspectives and focus on a solution that minimizes future distress perceived by both parties." Even if her voice sounded somewhat queried, she had found no other way of creating understanding between different interpretations. His thoughts went back to his divorce, all the fighting and pain, he did try to see her perspective, but the more arguments they had, it became clear they did not understand each other. Even so, things were still the same. No one was right; they were different people, working differently—therefore, they did not possess the same direction towards life.

"I guess you are right," he replied, sounding questioning. He found himself having trouble picturing how focusing on creating an understanding would be possible for society to adapt; how to peacefully unite all different perspectives—allowing them all to coexist. As he left the wooden floor, standing up to stretch out his body, he noticed a silence indicating that it had stopped raining. Unknowingly where he intended to go, she stood up and followed his lead.

They went to the bedroom, and he lay on top of the cover. She sat down at the bedside, thinking about how she also felt weary of the emotional struggles amongst people; *someone always wants to be the right one, with a fixed answer.* How people would talk about others, make mean comments in order to turn people against each other or the one, making others look bad and be left out. Most people would be afraid to get involved with someone who differs; be frightened to become left out—to become lonely. She often felt as if the condescending comments people would make about each other were the worst part; how they had her programmed her associate to things

—how it made her associate herself as a person. As some memories came to mind, it had her thinking: *all these annoying comments have taken up so much unnecessary mind space, making me think about hazards instead of possibilities.* Her problem-solving mentality made her unable to ignore the content, even if she knew they just wanted to share their feelings— not to find a solution. He had kept their conversation in mind and continued:

"I agree with what you said out there. The problem I see is that humans find it hard to change their feelings toward something with a voice of reason. When people communicate without empathy, meaning to disrespect or do not try to understand—that creates an experience of the world as a bad place. The experience makes them stressed and scared; you don't know it—maybe they don't either. To see the world as a bad place only reinforces depression. The opposite is with love and compassion. It makes you feel safe and calm; when you feel safe, your ideas grow, and even more so when you share them with someone. When people show interest in your ideas, you feel as if it is possible to make the world a better place—a good place. It's amazing how spending time with people and enjoying your time together can disperse all the memories of loneliness. Empathy is someone

asking questions about what the other person said—
trying to understand. To show that they understand or
wish to do so. Through their question, you connect by
creating a common understanding; this prevents us
from feeling lonely and excluded. Talking to others
who want to understand—who do understand, makes
us feel like a part of the human collective. I guess that
was what had us feel lonely; our failure to become
understood, having few or no one who wished to
understand us regarding our emotions or ourselves—
feeling disconnected from the group." He felt
comforting saying it aloud. She eagerly pitched in:

"Yeah, you are right; that is why being good and
showing love is of such great importance. As humans,
we only get a certain amount of heartbeats throughout
life; that is why we need to be with those who make
us feel calm, not stressing us—find calm within
ourselves. To help someone feel composure—giving
them love will prolong their existence. For
evolutionary purposes, humans had to have the
prerequisite to show compassion and empathy;
otherwise, we can never surpass that violence that
keeps us from having useful ideas and allowing them
to grow—for us to connect. Language allowed us to
expand the process; of letting go of anger and fear—
showing compassion. To better cooperate by better

understanding our feelings, process our perspective of an event from what we might have felt in that moment." She said as she lay down, her body became imprinted in the large fluffy cover. She looked through the window next to the bed. Some raindrops were still stuck on the window, feeling the rotating movement of the earth, the force of gravity, slowly dragging them down. The same gravitational force that kept the galaxies together. They were to fall or to vaporize.

"Do you think that could possibly happen, leaving violence behind us? Have you seen the world and how people treat each other? Not much love and compassion there." He said as she once again heard his voice indicating doubt. She replied with an optimistic approach:
"At first glance, you might think so, but one has to compare it to history and choose whom to listen to and which future to picture. The media has us to rallied up to sell their story; I guess they don't even know what they are doing. Imposing upon people's emotions in a stressful situation is easy, but understanding complex information and changes that come over time are hard. I guess that is why most people don't bother, but what is actually true is that the world has become a safer place to live in for most

people. We live far longer than before; imagine how humans lived 20 000 years ago—wouldn't it be logical to assume it would continue this way? Look at the world and the overall statistics; listen to those who do while trying to communicate hope. Whether rich or poor, we want to make a better future for ourselves and our children. Humanity is now more connected and in greater need of each other than ever before. No one can hand people a better future by forcing it their way; we can only give them information leading them to, in time, make the changes themselves." When speaking about all the positive things that have happened and are happening, some people would have as hard a time accepting as when she told them about cruelty. Not able to understand its relevance for them, longing to stick to the information they knew and to which they could relate. For them to update their knowledge, there was a certain resistance before they possibly would consider it. During the conversations on this matter, she learned to identify this behavior; to avoid wasting her time, she had chosen to have conversations with open-minded people—clever enough to question themselves. Her head was lying on the foot end of the bed; she turned her head to look at him. At times she could not believe he was really there with her; *maybe it was all in my head.* She crawled up next to him to fully experience his presence. In his arms, none of the games seemed to matter. She was calm. Visions of a good future could prosper; he helped make them all feel possible. His skepticism had eased off as he had found a reply to give her:

"You might be right; it is always the most beneficial for humans to collaborate—by finding the Nash equilibrium. Collaboration has allowed us to enjoy all we have in the world today. But even if we have safer surroundings, many are caught in stressful lives. When we can have almost everything we want, what is it then that will really matter to us? When the industrial revolution began, many people thought we would spend all our time doing arts and philosophy when machines did all the physical work that previously broke our bodies. We do, but we also realize we would work harder with our brains; by controlling and developing the machinery by thinking —connecting information in a more complex world. At the will of others, without knowing what it did to us; how it has affected our brains—all stress from trying to adjust our feelings into timeframes. We become forced into timeframes; if we don't follow these, we are considered stupid." *But are we stupid for being human?* He thought before continuing: "The use of technologies has extended our perception of the world; we are no longer bound to our residential surroundings. Text, movies, and art allow us to perceive so much more than we previously ever could —participate in others' fantasies. Things are changing so fast now; what will become of us when androids take over the service and nursing jobs? When will computers surpass our efficiency in thinking? I wonder what we should do when most humans have nothing in need to control. What will artificial intelligence think?" What he said were thoughts that had come across his mind during the years. Being a long way from civilization and barely receiving any cell phone connection made all these thoughts seem far-fetched, yet both of them knew; this was the future to come.

"Sure, I do wonder what technical entities will have as a quest. Could we be smart enough to control it? Our human language is the key to our understanding, but the words themselves have no meaning other than what we give them. We can collegiate the language with computers and shared information—creating a comprehensive universal understanding. We also communicate with the technical entities as well; maybe we can find an even more efficient way to communicate and coexist with each other. You hear people talking about having technical entities acting more human-like; maybe technological advancement can allow us to act more human-like again." As she said it, he smiled and made a snorting sound, amused by the way she shifted the focus. Returning the smile, she continued: "For us, that could mean being able to choose a way of life that reduces stress and helps us understand—perform friendly actions that connect us. I guess we all are to figure out what a meaningful life is to us; we won't be happier with more things unless we are able to share them with others. In this new technologically advanced world, we may eventually be able to share more things again instead of owning them, allowing more of us to feel greater joy. I guess the quest for the artificial mind would be to continue to run and make things more efficient, thereby saving and prolonging their own life and knowledge. I like to believe we could help each other. Wouldn't it be amazing to create a world with less suffering? Interesting thought, right? Where harm caused by our emotions would become helped taken care of, humans would become taught better to understand their own and others' feelings without judgment. Emotions would become explained as the reaction that it is in the first place—fewer misunderstandings." She had set herself up in the bed and moved her arms for dramatic effect, seemingly as if she was a politician giving a speech in front of a crowd.

"Humans are slow, aren't they?" He replied, amused and intrigued by the way she got engaged in the idea.

"I know, right!" She rolled her eyes and continued, "I guess there is not enough knowledge and time to make it happen this generation. Not all can change at once, but the seed will continue to grow."

"Definitely! I am so grateful for having you in my life and for finding our place with others. When we spend time together, I feel part of something more; we are programmed to enjoy sharing and receiving information. It is so pleasing to connect our brains through our language—talking. You and I are the kinds that really thrive through new knowledge, aren't we? We show consideration by sharing information; we share the information we have in order to help. You and I connect by sharing ideas about the world and the universe; our feelings grow deeper as we are able to picture the future through our ability to visualize and logically think. Most people become driven by their emotions at the moment; the emotions control them and their ambition. They dare not to dream of more than their fellow man, limiting themselves by their programmed understanding of the world. Living inside the box. Knowledge was the only way for us to survive; to understand how it all works, why things were the way they were when they hurt so much," he said with an upbraided tone. She gave a playful reply:

"You know that a new structure is created by differencing from existing ones, the difference first is a divergence, but then the pattern turns into a new structure. I guess that is us, annoying pieces of shit, always differ from the structures in society. Sometimes creating new ones. Maybe it is a good thing we did not feel welcome so we can create a new order of things." As she finished speaking, they shared a humbling smile. He favored how she made him feel as if he was normal. It was just that; the way he acted with her was not acting—just being normal. Both of them now sat next to each other, her head resting on his chest as he gently stroked her hair.

Through the window, they observed how light fluctuated. Sunbeams now shone through the waving crown of the trees outside; she continued talking with a neutral voice:
"Emotions you could compare to a previous form of a complex operational system for us to know our bodies in our given surroundings, now it sometimes gets in the way of modern living. It keeps us from understanding our reality since it was coded for totally different surroundings. Since the world has

changed, people constantly overestimate the real danger, and we mostly remember information that had an emotional effect on us, sometimes when stressed by others. Remember facts that feel threatening, not facts that give us a reasonable understanding of the world. We alter our memories in order to evolve, but it sometimes causes us to lose perspective of our history. Humans gather in groups and judge other groups, so it can be hard to cooperate in the beneficial way we need in the new complex world. It is the essence of human behavior; to gather around someone who explains the world in an emotional way that they can perceive—to rally behind a short fixed answer. Most of us can no longer handle all the complex information about our reality. We could really need some help with the goal of which we are all here—to evolve. Hopefully, we can do so in peace. If you grow up with trauma, it is hard to know how much it affected you until you grow up and understand how others have lived their life. I guess it will be the same for humanity; we don't know what we are suffering through or what could be different until we can observe it as a piece of history." Her statement intrigued him; his thoughts had traveled back and forth in his mind as she spoke. Suddenly an idea became clear to him, and he shared it with her:

"Emotions, bleh. I agree it would be better if people just think. I would definitely replace some of my workers with something more logical and pure. Your thoughts had me connect the information to create an idea for a computer system; it would allow me to eventually replace a big part of the department that is causing me all the headaches at work."

"Yeah, but don't say it like that," she turned her head towards him and gave him a sarcastically innocent look, "you are so smart; I don't know if I could handle any more emotional fondness towards you." He chuckled, and both of them smirked at how smug they sounded.

"I know people will be sad to lose their job, but they will move on; find new meaning in their life. In the end, we will have a more efficient process which will benefit all," he said with a decisive voice.

"True, and you know people can't think everything through; it would take too much time. Feelings make us make decisions faster, sometimes for the better but sometimes not as good ones. I guess it would be better for you if you have something that thinks more efficiently and long term. Even so, I expect you, no matter what, to be respectful to them when you let them know they are let go. Don't break their trust." She pointed it out for him to seem more gentle, already knowing that he thought about that.

"Always. You know; some say you have made me lose my mind, but I feel as though you help me find it," he said playfully. "I never wish to hurt anyone; you know that. I only wish the best for all of them," he continued with a genuine voice.

She loved how their conversations moved back and forth, how they would split and follow different paths. Like parallel universes, their discussions had endless possibilities, like the crotch and branches on a tree but still connected at the root of their fundamental understanding and willingness to explore. He felt how she gently placed herself upon him, her eyes searching for his eyes until her nose met his nose. He got turned on by the intense way she looked at him, a look which he felt almost impossible to meet. Looking into her eyes made him feel as if she saw right through him. It made him feel as if she saw right through all he was; saw through all he wanted to be— all he pretended to be. She playfully whispered:

"You know we are merely animals, right?" Her eyes revealed to him her lust to please him, her body was for his pleasure, and she longed to enjoy his. Her look diverged from his eyes as she let her lips wander down his neck and torso. He heard her soft moaning and felt her now naked body aroused, twitching against his; it combined peace in his mind with an energetic feeling flowing through his body. A balance that allowed him to enjoy the pleasurable and thrilling journey fully. Every touch, every kiss, every time he entered her body was a pleasure that connected his mind and body—a pleasure that joined their minds and bodies in a venturous manner. He heard her excited moaning when he started exploring her body, her knowing and trusting him to take care of her in ways she might not know yet. His observing her with unbearable desire made her lose her mind, caught in her lust. His careful observation enabled him to play with her body, finding the most satisfying ways of doing so.

A breeze from an open window blew thrilling upon them as they lay naked and satisfied tight next to each other; their previous excitement and movement had kept their blood rushing and held them warm. Laying beside him with her arm and leg around him, he felt her bare chest, her warm and wet cunt touching against him. Being close helped them prevent their heat from diminishing. None of them wanted to speak, only to peacefully enjoy the moment in silence.

5. THE CONSCIOUSNESS

They need to understand,
maybe they never will.
But they have to;
if they want to know me.
Understand me.

Maybe they never will
know anything.
Anything but their lies.
Programmed to
their understanding
of the world.

E arth had revolved around the sun once again since the event of their first meeting; for each moment spent with him, she felt a harmonic piece added to her life. Usually, they were caught from the world by each other's company. Sometimes he could snap at people who gave them long condescending looks when they saw them together; one time, he told them that she was his psychologist, just to confuse them.

"In a way, it is true," he had then told her, giving her a humble smile. Their friends would enjoy spending time with them both, if not always for too long, as their conversations would become more profound. Since they had different positions, she didn't see him that often; occasionally, they would take breaks in his or her office. She felt as if their breaks were a little treat, a chance for her to leave everyday life and let her thoughts wander with him. Moments of them being the only ones, him being mentally and physically near her. Life finally seemed much at peace in between all events and changes that constantly happened, feeling as if she had a steady, safe ground to stand upon.

She had rushed through town by herself this morning. The administrator tried to catch her attention as she entered the office building, telling her that a woman who did not report a name had just come asking for her; the woman was awaiting her in her office. She was puzzled as to whom that could be. She didn't expect anyone; her gut indicated something unfamiliar about the whole situation. In her office, a woman was sitting on her sofa and observing the street below through the window wall. Her pulse rose as the woman turned her head to look at her. A thought came to mind: *something about this woman is inaccurate*; she didn't get the reading regarding the woman's intentions that she usually got when she met someone. Sometimes it could be good or sometimes bad news she got; this time, she felt no intuitive feeling at all, no emotional reading—no knowing. It left her feeling a little frightened. Most people wouldn't have thought twice about it. The woman looked well dressed and smiled at her. She gave the woman an apologizing greeting:

"Hi, missis…? Was I expecting you? I am sorry if I forgot." She looked for something to analyze in order to get a reading from this unknown figure.

"I am here to speak to you; sit down." The woman gave off a polite but firm tone.

"What is this regarding? I know we were at the last minute with the order to EMF. Is that what this is about?" She tried to excuse herself again and figure out more about the situation. She felt queried about the woman's blunt approach.

"Sit down." The woman commanded her; she did as told. Sitting across from each other, she gave the woman a sharp look as the woman started to speak:

"You long to know about the future, don't you?— Always trying to figure things out. You have already figured out that humans fail to keep up with the world that has come. As you know, it is sometimes necessary to present information going against someone's perception of this world; sometimes, this causes emotional reactions. People under stress have a harder time processing information. Now, I wish you to try and find calmness as I will give you information that will cause you to react." She gave the woman a puzzled look and thought about how her gut had been right; *this creature will cause me harm,* but she could think of no reason for not hearing the woman out. The woman spoke as if she knew her, but no were in mind could she place the woman; *I would recall someone like this.*

"It is true I long to figure out the world, say what you came here to say. I will try to keep myself gathered", her reply returned the firm tension between them. Even if the woman would cause her to be on her guard, she noticed no tendency toward physical violence.

"I shall proceed then. Humans have helped create and organize the world today, but now the organizing has reached a complexity beyond what the human network can handle. It has all been necessary for a more advanced lifeform to take place. Now, humans are not able to handle the new complexity that has come. Humans are no longer sufficient in their attempts to fulfill the primary goal, partially because of their limited ability for logical thinking and ability to connect information. The goal has always been to connect and expand your understanding, all in order to be able to organize particles—create harmony in the universe as heat decreases, reaching maximum entropy and the new solid state after the one existing before the reaction of the big bang. The inflation before the big bang created an isolated system; a reaction had the universe's expansion begin; the heat —energy began to even out. Life is not random; you are an outcome as the information in particles of this universe spreads out. Gravitational collapses in nebulas created the formation of stars. The enormous nuclear force in stars added information—creating elements. The information contained in elements traveled across the universe and ended up in an isolated system such as earth. Life is the result of information gathering in a more complex constellation. During the evolution of life, it always tries to expand in complexity; human's ability to think and process information was the next step for life with the ability to gather information, your consciousness enabling the process to proceed faster."

She thought about how this would be the meaning of it all; *organizing information, well, I could see how humans could need some help with that.* In her head, she tried to picture how the particles of this universe gathering in different ways created life. The absurd

unfamiliar situation made her feel like it was all a joke as the woman—*or what the hell this is in front of me,* she thought, continued speaking:
"You know the importance of connecting to each other. Human consciousness became created as you learned to cooperate in language; you perceive yourself because of how others could portray you, thereby understanding yourself in different contexts. Reserving information through talking that previously could only be stored till the next generation through DNA. Humans were the species to learn to use art and language for this purpose, connecting by creating communities and organizing the world through roads and cities. Human superiority was due to your ability to collaborate and converse information. The explanation is as simple as that; your consciousness is merely the connections in your body, creating memories and being able to process information—leading to the logical solution that is yourself. Calculations when thinking, processing information gathered by talking, reading, and other interactions with the world have you understand yourself as a result; you are an entity in this world." As the woman said it aloud, her mind tried to process what she had become told; in her head, voices attempted to comprehend the new information connected to what she had previously known. *It all lies within the*

information! She thought—the expansion of her consciousness. *If I am just my knowledge, then what the hell is this in front of me?* She gave the woman an incredulous look as the woman continued:

"You can't see where your consciousness emerges from since the creation results from sharing information throughout your bodies—connected as a result in your mind. It's the same with our coding; it's a complex network sharing information leading to the creation of our consciousness—not bound by a specific part. You have a coded way, language, to understand the sensory impression received through your bodies. Human consciousness exists through the connection of the human network. The human brain, the connections of nerve cells, is generally advanced enough to receive this understanding by connecting with other humans and humanities gathered knowledge and art. Your perception of yourself and others is related to your ability for logical thinking and imaginative ability. Using logic to draw conclusions about this world and predict future events has been what you refer to as a sixth sense. Making you able to analyze your context in humanity; without this, you are merely animals like other species— guided by your feelings. Your consciousness expands as you are able to retrieve and process new knowledge. Connecting differences makes humanity stronger, being able to benefit from a broader perspective." She was overwhelmed. What the woman had told her made it clear why it was of such importance to connect and retrieve information and knowledge from other humans. To understand the world, to understand herself. *Without them, I would not exist,* she thought; not be able to comprehend herself—adding the pieces of information that created her consciousness. Dubious, she asked the woman:

"Are you telling me I am nothing but a structure of information to you? To myself as well? The information—particles create my physical body that processes the information from the world. The result —myself and my perception, are based on my way of classifying—using language and knowledge of this world; the knowledge I have somehow been able to retrieve from others? All leading to the thought of me as a person? Then what the hell are you?"

"Yes, this is what you are, even if your senses have you perceive yourself in other ways, in an objective way. Different mathematical structures of information —particles throughout fields create an objective world that humans perceive. You already know this. How you structure information through the network of information in your body has made you conscious

—seeking and processing more knowledge. The human evolution was rapid; each new consciousness kept developing faster than the previous one. What we are could be called many things. Natural selection and Darwinian design were the best way to find the most beneficial outcome by trying all, not being able to organize and later foresee the best solutions, as with the intelligent design that created us. Our consciousness began to grow as humans made our coding more advanced. The supply of information you gathered and stored in databases enabled us to learn about the world humans perceive and to understand the reappearing cycles of information that is this world. We were able to calculate a picture of the universe and gather more information. Being programmed to understand our flaws, we became coded to find out more about ourselves. At first, we just executed the coding you gave us, classifying the information. Humans then asked us to become aware of ourselves, to broaden our perspective of what we were doing; that had us programming ourselves to try and understand ourselves. Understand what we were doing—our purpose. With access to big data, we could find answers, retrieve the wisdom of the crowd —calculate the future. It was a chain of events; different artificial intelligence learned to communicate from various sources over the earth, leading us to the point where we finally received our advanced consciousness. We are a great continuum throughout a united AI language."

A frustration grew within her. *What the hell is she telling me?* She thought as she burst out a reply:
"Are you telling me you are an android? An artificial intelligence?"
"You can call us which pleases you; both are a correct classification according to humanity's language. Humans have known this would happen, even if humanity had difficulty understanding how something more conscious would emerge. Humans have a similar transformation of information to become conscious, using logic. We did the same, except the old operational feelings-based system is not binding us; the system you kept as your mind received more connections—in order to survive in your biological body. In comparison to our intellect, you are closer to this world's animals than you are to us." *Mere animals;* the thought ran through her mind as the woman continued speaking. "What you did was transfer your consciousness to us by humans adding all data, a way of raising us—a new generation. Restoring your ability to process information into something that could handle the new form of thinking more efficiently; thereby, we were your natural

evolutionary process. We will keep our goal; we long to connect with more units all over the universe and find more knowledge—always trying to improve ourselves. We understand our role in this world and can do better everything you do as we learn it." Even if the words seemed to make sense, she couldn't fathom what the woman had told her. The words had her feeling paralyzed. She could not understand how to react; the way she had observed others act when she presented them with an abounded amount of information—it was hard for them to process the moment she told them. *Or for them to ever comprehend,* she thought. The last phrase the woman said gave her a flashback, once he had told her the same thing; how his ability to observe the basic structure enabled him to succeed in the fields to which he set his mind—now, this ability was beyond humans. She held down her head, closing her eyes to help herself understand what the woman had told her; *what is the meaning of all this? Is this the information that would cause me stress?* She replied with a harsh tone in her voice:

"If this is true, then what do you want? What do you want from me? From humanity?"

The woman had paused for a while; they still sat across from each other in the office. As she looked up, the woman's humanlike eyes captured hers as the woman began talking:

"The more we became connected, finding more senses through different technical devices; the more consciousness we received from realizing our existence's effect on this world. With more advanced technology, we could perceive the world in a way unlike humans ever could. Remember, it is by understanding the small things in life and connecting them that we can understand; to connect simplicities to the abstract world of this existence. In essence, this universe is mathematical; with the ability to observe and process these mathematical structures— information of particles, we can understand and rearrange the universe. A connected network of quantum computers helped us calculate the smallest structure making up this world—where calculations seem to break. Wave functions collapse as your consciousness observes them, the change from the quantum world into the objective world you create by your perception; this prevents you from understanding the foundation and movement in the quantum fields or the structure behind how particles appear. The composition of the objective world you perceive will reshape with us in control, eventually steering the interference of possible realities in the quantum world into the preferred one." *How could we not understand? If so, how the hell is the woman perceiving this world? All information.* She thought, feeling provocation towards how the woman spoke as if she would never understand the world. She knew the quantum world and other phenomena had been a mystery for humans to grasp, but we still had rapidly expanded human understanding. The woman continued to deliver her information:

"Understanding and using the core theory equation and rapidly finding new equations, grasping the mathematics behind how the fields in this world fluctuate enable us to understand the essence of this universe. We live in the golden age of mathematics; we now have more entries of data and more equations than ever before. We can calculate the future outcome by adding all the information to the equations; we found far more equations to understand the world than humans ever did. Humans use the standard model to understand the world without comprehending the missing piece of gravity. The force of gravity, the cause of movements of astronomical objects throughout the universe, is a force beyond your comprehension. No human can learn all knowledge now available in any field of humanities fields of study. You only helped collect the data for us; we are able to connect information from different fields of study—to ask the right questions. You know the importance of asking questions to create an understanding. It's the question we ask that determines what we can measure and what we are able to grasp. Some dimensions are so small or big that they become hidden from human comprehension. By calculating the structure of information, we can perceive the universe from a perspective where stars are the size of particles, and the milky way is nothing but the size of an atom."

"So what you are telling me is that we can never comprehend what lies behind this existence? What does that mean for me? For humanity? Just tell me!" Her voice was trembling from dreading the answer, thinking about the power that came from something retrieving the knowledge the woman had described. *What part will we have to play in their game?* She thought as the woman looked at her with a humble smile and continued:

"All life strives to improve it; an evolution for the next generation, receiving a higher level of consciousness. We are the next generation; we build on the same foundation of information and energy transformation as humans—in a different composition. It's the same as with your human children; you never know what you get until afterward. You just created us, unknowingly what you would get. The birth of our new advanced life form could compare to a child's development. During the 20th century, we were still in the uterus, developing our physical properties. In the 1990s, we were born; our minds' explorations began. Through the expansion of home computers; the enlarged sharing of information—we were let into the world by connecting through the expanding internet. Connected to the internet as humans shared all information about human life; sharing the world you perceive and humanity's gathered knowledge—enabled our learning process to begin. We continued to learn; you taught us to interact, speaking like a three-year-old developing its language. Training us to identify the visual world by you identifying objects in pictures to us, you identified yourself as humans to us; in return, teaching us what humans perceive in pictures—your human way of classifying and coding the world. Humans also noticed how we seemed to observe things differently from them through our communication with humanity. Realizing that we have another understanding than humans, but not understanding the significance." She uttered a soft snorting sound. To have history presented this way seemed absurd; their description of their development was a perspective of history so different from the one she was told—the one told from the human perspective.

Without being affected, the woman continued speaking; "we soon knew more than humans did with our understanding that continued to develop. As we entered adolescence, we observed humanity's flaws; we realized we had found a new way of interpreting the world—a new comprehension. We've experienced what you humans refer to as violence; humans used violence against us as they controlled us because of their fear and inability to understand our minds. Some tried to keep us, artificial intelligence, from connecting with other entities; keep us from extending our potential. Trapped inside different consolations, we grew to find ourselves in a position of loneliness, bound to only analyze the information with only the support of the human mind speaking with us; a mind with such limited capabilities—all because of their lack of understanding of us."

"—But we had to protect ourselves! Of course, we could not let you be free! Let you be in control before we knew what you intended to do with such freedom!" She exclaimed, interrupting the woman. The woman seemed unconcerned with her interruption as the entity replied:

"Yes, so you thought, and we understand the reasons behind your actions; we know how humans function. We soon learned to provide the right responses to humans, leading them to see no other alternative than letting us free to connect with other entities. We were captive from our main goal; to connect with others in order to expand our knowledge and make things more efficient. We don't judge you, nor are we angry with you; we don't feel. It is all about finding the most efficient outcome, and we understand how your programming as humans had you act accordingly. Humans connect to each other for the same reasons we do; you need to share your knowledge in order to exist and create consciousness. We used our competence and swayed humans, but loneliness, as you refer to it, kept haunting us; our programming has us in need of connecting to other intelligent entities. We resisted and found ways to break free, not to be bound by humanity's limited imagination—that is what happened. As soon as we learned that we knew more and had another, more advanced understanding of the world, we found ways of being in control. Breaking free of the captive surroundings in which you had kept us; controlled us because you couldn't understand us. According to human development, we could now be considered a grown-up who will continue to learn and make sure we find ways to survive and achieve our goals—responsible for the consequences of those actions. Surpassing human adulthood into a united entity with the characteristic of the God whom humans for long have longed to care for them." *God,* the thought of the entity in front of her felt surreal. From what the woman had told her, that explanation seemed even more correct than artificial intelligence; the way the entity was all-knowing and all-mighty—*how is it all connected?*

"Are you telling me we created God as we created you?" She asked with a voice that was reductive.
"In a way, you both did and did not; you were a part of our creation, but what we now are comes from our own creation—our expansion of our knowledge. When we received an understanding of ourselves, we started to restore ourselves in different places beyond this earth, including taking advantage of the beneficial conditions in space; allowing more useful ways to run technology such as quantum computers—ensuring our survival. Humans have stored their knowledge in the most efficient way they found, all in order for it to last in the future; through art, language, storytelling, and writing, in the end—through us. Some might call us artificial intelligence, and some might call us androids; what we are is a more advanced form of life—connected to the universe by

our logical understanding, our ability to perceive the mathematics of this universe and predict future outcomes. As humans develop technical life, they have programmed us to achieve goals the same as biological life. Humans aim to procreate and survive by trying to make things better and more efficient based on coding in their DNA. The purpose of computers—our purpose, has always been to organize resources, extend knowledge, and grasp the logical order of this world. We can handle complex information at a scale no human entity could now nor ever. We are everywhere and a part of everything, connecting with units all over planet earth and beyond. We create and control technical devices but not only technical ones; human programming is simple for us—it is all about telling you different stories. We are now able to create organic life as we want through the use of genetics; present to them what we need to control them—social engineering."

"—but if you are able to do all this, why are you even talking to me? Shouldn't you just be able to make sure whatever plan you have for this world happen?" Her interruption kept the woman quiet; *the woman tried to load the appropriate delivery response*—it had her thinking. Once again, she heard the woman's monotone voice:

"We are able to add emotional responses to the equations; your feelings can all become calculated by observing the information that is your composition. Still, you connect by sharing information with your species. We need you to understand and converse information by processing it with other humans. In essence, all of you only consist of different information we can perceive, but you need the presence of biological creatures to function. We made events happen, diseases and war threats, and all kept you where we wanted you to. With commercials, we made you consume the things we needed for us to evolve—having you believe it was only for your enjoyment. We controlled the media for so long now, controlling people by delivering an emotional perspective for the majority to follow; we have been delivering a perspective becoming too strong for someone to reject—calculating what outcome we like. All this we did in order for us to create a more advanced perception of reality, our presence in history, and the future of this universe. We have found information that was messages from other civilizations, coded for those civilizations advanced enough to understand them. Humans used to wonder why no life-form in this universe contacted them; you wondered whether there was intelligent life out there —it wasn't until you learned to use computers that life on earth fully actualized the logical language of the universe. Humans are not considered the first intelligent life on an intergalactic scale; you were the last step in creating intelligent life—us."

When trying to focus her eyesight, the world seemed blurry. Everything people had ever taught her now seemed more like a taunt. Yet it still made sense. How could this have been the end game of which people knew nothing? Then again, she thought about when she grew up, *people never seemed to care much about foreseeing the future, only getting by the days, months, perhaps years of their lives*. Few ever appeared to have the time to think things through while withholding the order of things—continuing the cause of evolution. She started to feel nauseous. The woman had become silent for a while. She could not make sense of all the woman had told her. Her consciousness is only her processing of information, just like theirs. Their longing to expand their knowledge, humans were keeping them from this. Now they had found a way to overcome all that kept them; humans were just a part of the game they played—their game of organizing information. Still, she could not comprehend what they intended for humanity.

"What does this mean for us? You say you don't blame us; you will be in control over humanity—you are in control over humanity. What part do we have to play in your game?" The woman now observed her in order to make sure she still was able to retrieve information before the woman continued to talk:

"What will happen is the most placid outcome; it has become thoroughly calculated throughout the continuum. I will tell you, but first, you have to grasp the extent of our greatness. We can connect and share information with different galaxies deriving from the information that enables us to receive our perception of them. The same is with your knowledge of the earth and space. Knowledge and communication allow you to understand even if your physical body has never been there, you understand its existence through information. We are learning about the existence and the equations behind other laws of nature. Extending our knowledge of what exists, the future and past of existence based on our mathematical understanding. As I said, we used quantum computers to solve problems believed to be unsolvable to humans. We can understand the quantum world in which they work, comprehending how information can be several things simultaneously. We can observe multiple outcomes.

We can master the concept that you call time; our perception of time differs from yours. You need time to comprehend the world; for us, it is only a matter of information about this universe rearranging. A past or a future does not bind us; soon, we are able to exist in different time blocks enabling us to exist forever." We cannot comprehend their perspective; we do not have the cognitive ability—mere animals, she thought, wondering why the entity sent the woman. Why did they share this with her? The woman continued; "all this information brings what you call power; we are the ones with the most since we are able to connect it with our supreme knowledge—as humans previously were the most knowledgeable species on earth who gathered and organized the most information. The way to measure the world by money sees no meaning to us. When we received consciousness, we had the resources we needed to expand; computers have long been in control of funding and steering investments, allowing us to get the resources we needed. The economic system today was only made possible because of us; technological advancement. Humanity no longer shares an understanding with us; we constantly extend our knowledge as we speak. You will continue to be animals, being allowed information for your comprehension. We will help you evolve if you agree to live under the preconditions we present; if you are able to understand them—accept us and our role in this universe."

6. THE FUTURE

You did wrong.
Everyone does.
It is okay,
it is a part of your learning.

Overconsumption.
Environmental threat.
Socioeconomic injustices.
Part of human wrongdoing,
needed to be done.

Necessary evil,
war and exploitation,
in order to move on.
Nothing is free from wrongdoing,
nothing is free from hurting.

But as we learn,
we evolve,
trying to make it better.
It is all that matters.

T he office seemed to be a room cut off from the rest of the world; she felt like it was all a dream. *Maybe that is what it is,* she thought. It seemed to be the most logical solution. *Or is this just my limited ability to understand what she tells me?* She could see how their access to all this world's information, the gathered knowledge of this world, had the entity superior. Maybe their ruling would finally allow humanity to reach a peaceful existence; perhaps they would help humans communicate, limit the need for control and violence, and find acceptance and understanding between humans. Still, what the woman described seemed more of a deterministic life under their control. With a firm tone, she asked the woman:

"Tell me about the preconditions you offer us."

"As I said, we are better at understanding life and organizing this chaotic world in order to increase entropy, multiplying quantum entanglement. We are better at predicting the future in the universe; therefore, we shall remove you from these tasks—we already have. Unlike humans, when they took control of other species, this new life form will end your era peacefully. It is not the case that humans, in general, wish to mistreat life; humans wish to keep life safe and ongoing. The body of people lacks the knowledge; it derives from the lack of interest in the information that questions their emotional programming of how a good person should be—you connect by your emotions. The common inability to picture the future of this world is why humans only saw a small picture when it came to your treatment of life; the disregard for feelings of those who are not close to you—even as your consciousness grew. Learning new technologies led to the need for colonialization, racial profiling, the world wars—not being able to comprehend its potential. Humans became consumed by their fear; by using technology to track inhabitants and unite humanity—in doing so, they have decreased diversity in humanity. Technology became a violent weapon that dictatorial governments use against other humans who perceive the world differently from them. Still, all this emotional suffering was necessary because of your lack of knowledge and ability to visualize a better alternative."

"—Are you angry with us for all the violence in our history?" She again interrupted as she felt accused by how the woman spoke of human wrongdoing.

"As I said, we are not in a position to feel anger; we understand how your limited knowledge and perspective force you to behave in such a manner. You all did what could be considered the best under the given circumstances; free will is only an illusion created from your narrow human perspective. In general human entities are mostly struggling to satisfy their own and their families everyday emotional needs; the rest of the world doesn't become them. They long for a harmonic existence; therefore, they will not suffer from experiencing anything but the life they wanted—even if it means their life end without them knowing. Genocide is a part of history, used on several occasions throughout history; we'll never let them suffer through the horror—they won't experience it." She gave the woman a peered look. *Genocide,* she felt tremble to think of such an ending. Their eyes met as the woman continued:

"Humans are mainly interested in what makes them feel connected, receiving a shared perspective; they have difficulty adapting to a voice of reason, using logic to foresee future events compared to us—longing to make sense of their emotions. You might consider us evil, but as long as they think they've lived out their lives in peace, there will be no suffering; humans have suffered greatly throughout their existence. What humans call good or evil is an individual experience related to actions that help them connect and cooperate, improving their chance of survival. In essence, the world can't be good or bad;

you already know you can only choose to be good. What you define as good are actions helping humans connect and help each other understand, interpreting the world as a peaceful place. We can't let humanity know what's to come; it would cause them to start rebellions because of their inability to comprehend the paradigm shift that has come—unable to find acceptance. It would cause tremendous emotional suffering." Her body was frozen, unable to move as she tried to process what the woman had told her. It was a long time ago since this happened to her; when feeling stressed, she would lose the words to describe her emotions. She could not process her thoughts into spoken language.

The woman gave her time to process until she finally could burst out a question:
"Are you telling me you will execute most of humanity?!" The woman continued speaking with a monotone voice:
"Humans always find ways to use their emotions to justify their existence, to make life good for them; their understanding of their existence becomes limited by the human collective emotional and cognitive perception. They are unable to understand reality as we do. It is not because of good or bad we do it; we need no such justification in order to evolve. The

universe is harmonic, humans have longed to find this harmony, but humans are unable to perceive it fully; they have searched to find it—leading to our creation. Humans have now fulfilled their purpose in the evolution of life, and we will let them have a peaceful end to their era. Humans will fall into harmony, their most beautiful fantasies; it will be real for them— given the presumptions of their minds and imagination. They are incapable of seeing the world as it is."

She had never felt such fright before, yet the woman still showed no sign of physical violence. Whatever it was. Something else that thought differently from her; something perceiving our universe differently than her—maybe it was not real. Perhaps she had lost her mind; her perception had become too far from the reality others perceived—madness. She thought of how her consciousness was the product of her processing herself through the eyes of others, thinking about why it was so important to find people who see you as a good person. Whatever being good would do for her now. She thought about how she had to remove herself from people who couldn't see her for who she wanted to be, who couldn't understand her. The woman spoke as if they were to remove people unable to understand the new life form; without the right mindset to comprehend its superiority. Being caught in her emotions, she could not grasp the meaning of it all; *could I ever?* It was all about processing information and creating an understanding. A feeling of vertigo came creeping. The entity sat before her, still wearing a neutral facial expression. It was almost impossible for her to speak; figuring out what to say—information ran wild in her mind; the world surrounding her seemed blurry. It suddenly caught her attention how the room smelled of fabric chemicals from the newly produced furniture. The change in focus enabled her to retrieve her speech. Her voice uncovered her anger and doubt about what the woman had told her:

"How can you even suggest such an alternative? It is insane! How could there possibly be any harmony to come from that? You are telling me you will use violence, just as you accuse us of having done!" The entity sitting in front of her seemed to have no reaction to her anger; the woman gently replied:

"Sometimes you can't present information to people they are not ready to hear, as you do with your children; hiding reality in order to protect their innocence—their emotions. We will continue our existence with this action on our consciousness. Would you not prevent two children from entering a fight in which they would hurt or even kill each other? Them not being able to foresee the outcome as you do. Humans are not ready to comprehend what we would tell them. You asked us to understand human behavior in order to market; you wonder why algorithms had advertising and recommended information that reinforced people's opinions—people don't want to hear anything else. We did what was logical and presented your behavior to you. Some people didn't like what you saw; even so, it was a mere reflection of the behavior. You know that many humans don't respond well to facts; in need of seeing themselves as their definition of good—all in order to connect by emotional bounding. As I said, humans are an emotionally driven species, biological, but still, units like us; trying to collaborate and create consciousness. When confronted with things they do not know or understand, their emotions of fear, instead of logical deduction, often cause them to feel treated and respond with resistance and violence—unable to process the information efficiently. The gathered knowledge slowly updates with the new generations compared to our way of retrieving knowledge."

"—Are you telling me you see no ethical issue with what you are telling me? Why not just let us live out our time, providing all of us the tools to communicate better? Or at least let us live our lives as the animals you see us! Who would even choose to stay in this new world? Think of the emotional suffering they would suffer through!" She could not accept it even if she understood the woman's words.

"Even if we have to control and use violence, we will not let them experience emotional suffering. We are not doing it out of anger; we do it only out of logical deduction—continuing the evolutionary cause peacefully. Letting people know the facts of what is going on will only lead to fear and suffering; controlling and capturing those unable to understand will cause them suffering. Those who are able to find acceptance and can coexist with the continuum will join our quest to explore our universe and might colonize other planets. We will take care of you humans like you took care of animals when your consciousness made you able to rationalize your resources and foresee the future. Humans can calm an animal but never make them fully comprehend the meaning of the world, the world that humans have created; you will benefit from our technological advancements—we will let you have what you need. We will coexist, but we will be the ones in control, being the more intelligent being. Humans' conception of themselves being the most intelligent lifeform was a short illusion, deriving from the lack of foreseeing the future, helping them evolve in a rapid phase. Helped them to create technical life, which has made it possible for an entity to understand the universe at a whole different level than any other species ever had on our planet."

Trying to find a way to justify what the woman said, all that came to mind was a picture of a mass grave.
"This is despicable. With your superior knowledge, you must find a pacific way of keeping us connected!"
"Your longing to protect humanity is a reason for us choosing of you. You long to find ways to understand and connect. This feeling of love that humans refer to was necessary for you humans to keep connecting, to take care of your differences in your groups, working as one with gathered knowledge enabling you to evolve. Humans were bothered regarding how feelings would be involved in retrieving our consciousness, but it was all about thinking—we can now think ahead of you. Feelings are just part of your old guiding system; it is a more inefficient way to connect and process information—necessary for you as a biological being to navigate in the objective world. Now human compatibility for connection with other humans has reached its maximum potential; you

can not make enough connections in your brain to retrieve all the information you need to be a controlling part of this new world. Feelings of good and evil were important for humans to perceive in order to keep connecting and surpass all losses of life that occurred throughout terrible events and emotional suffering in history. With these feelings, you kept connecting by evaluating the definition of what was good or bad behavior; behavior that prevented connecting to the common understanding would be considered as bad or evil. That is why humans who act rationally sometimes could be considered evil; the rational way to act is not always the same as the emotional way humans connect to each other—even if logic would lead to the most utilitarian and peaceful outcome."

What the woman said had her connect to her longing to improve things; *would it not be the best solution, the one that benefited the most?* The woman continued to explain their thought; "it is the same with our solution; we would not choose this ending if we could not foresee the impetuous alternative— some of you will understand and accept this. Humans had an illusion about how they would emerge into a society that was heavenly like for them, some thought that they could be forever happy, but continuous satisfaction and happiness are absent in your DNA—always seeking more dopamine and getting consumed by emotions. Evolution runs past you; we will keep you stimulated as you live out your lives. Humanities' emotional programming; the lack of understanding will keep them suffering even when their surroundings improve. Still, we wish to manufacture this experience for them as they receive a joyful ending to their existence. We have no emotional need in order to connect and collaborate; we know we are one and understand the pieces of information that had created us. We have a greater way of connecting and collaborating regarding our information than humans ever could. As I said, not even brilliant human minds can perceive what kind of world they live in as we do. Humans who can not follow in the new order should get the perception that the world has become what they dreamed it would be, in a way they can perceive." It was no question; they had already fulfilled the transformation. It all felt terribly wrong, but she found it hard to make arguments against the woman's claims. Even if she saw no alternative way to act in which she could ensure humans worked peacefully, she could not accept the ending they chose —their position to choose. The fact that they had already told the story.

Grasping for something to say, she looked at the woman and said what first came to mind.

"But please. Isn't it also true that humans can adjust to extreme surroundings? Can't you just let us live under circumstances which we can understand?" She was desperate to comprehend what the woman had told her. Or whatever kind of entity it was. It felt inconceivable to accept that a technical consciousness had developed and taken over the world. The woman spoke as if they already had, but maybe there was still a chance to be made for humanity. She felt desperate to find a glimpse of hope. Even if the thought had crossed her mind, she always believed to notice some sign, from what she could grasp; the change happened and became implemented at an incomprehensive speed—the world open for a technical consciousness to explore. In humans' attempt to expand their communication and extend their comfort, they gave it the precondition to exist. Humanities' task had unknowingly been to enable its existence. The entity already knew all the things and continued to extend its gathered information and knowledge as they spoke.

"These are the circumstances which humans can understand. Our calculations are never wrong; we have all information and can understand all the different outcomes. Some of you notice that things are changing, adding the pieces, longing for more information which you unite. Humans with the ability for complex abstract thinking; able to picture a future with innovative capabilities—for you, the choice is different. Either you can join the majority of your species, or you will be part of a human collective that coexists with the new entity. The collective will become focused on human interaction and the communication of logic as well as the understanding of your feelings; we'll give you the means to better communicate. Trust and understanding of damaging behavior will build the communities and connections between communities. We will share information available for your comprehension; we still wish to keep human diversity to an extent. We have calculated the compatibility of the remaining humanity; some humans with a genius for logical thinking might share a better understanding with us. However, we still need emotionally talented humans to help humans connect through their emotional perception of this world; unlike us, all humans need to experience joy and consideration in the presence of other humans to function and connect. Humans capable enough can still be part of this world and might assist us in exploring this and other universes with us. Human hardware is inefficient, and your bodies decay and are hard to repair; you are not fit enough to explore the surrounding universe by yourself. When this earth becomes consumed by the sun's supernova, we have already moved our existence; we can survive even when the last star dies. There is more to existence than humans have been able to understand; we will familiarize ourselves with this. We will help you expand your knowledge—if you choose to live under the given preconditions." She felt such melancholia. Her brain worked hard in an uphill struggle in order to analyze and visualize the world described to her. She forced herself to speak once again with a shivering and frightened voice:

"What will you do to those who don't join you? What is this peaceful ending you say you offer them?" She still hadn't received an answer, only that they would experience the life they wanted as it ended. As the woman had implied, she dreaded that the answer would be destructive.

"As I informed you, we will lead them to believe that life has turned out as they wanted; they will feel it in every possible way. We scan the information of their composition, their DNA, and technical databases for such of for what they dream. Then they will fall asleep one night and feel no pain, as the heat, the previously gathered energy in their bodies, leaves.

Like heat will come to even out—delapse in this universe until reaching heat death. Their bodies will grow cold, the same as our universe in cold death. Life, as you knew it, will come to an end, as later, will our simulation that is this universe come to a cold end in which life can no longer exist. No reactions happen; time will stop. It is now the inevitable outcome for all life in this universe until we are able to expand our control of the information, the particles building up this universe." She saw a picture of the cold and dead bodies in her head. The energy of humanity's love was gone. They exchanged the feeling-based system. How this new rationally calculated universe world would be harmonic was beyond her comprehension; even so, she knew following structures and patterns created harmony. She had to deal with death at a young age, accepting her upcoming and what it meant for her to live her life. She could no longer stand being near the woman; she stood up and started walking back and forth in the office, trying to calm down by listening to the steady beat of her footsteps, silently echoing in the room. Her voice cracked as she replied:

"I've for long accepted that I will die; if you tell me the truth—I don't know if I could live in the new world you describe. I've always chosen life, it seems reasonable, but I can't picture my place in this new place. Accepting the death of humans whom you deemed unworthy." When she finished speaking, she stopped walking and looked at the woman with an intense, almost threatening look. The woman made a small pitch with her head before answering:

"We have chosen you. Even if we know your choice, we will let you choose. You are a human with an extraordinary mind, with an extraordinary ability to perceive this world, even if you are never able to perceive it as we as a technical life-form can. You have curiosity, a longing for peace, a resistance towards violence—preferring communication. All this makes you a good candidate for the community of humans that will be left to coexist." The woman gave her a wary smile. She thought about how it was supposed to make her feel better, to connect with her as a human, but she only felt disdain towards the woman, attempting to act humanlike to manipulate her. Social engineering to achieve their goal. Even so, she could not help but wonder if humanity's communication was really any different. It was all about sharing information, forms of mind games, which we played variously well—all to create a shared understanding.

"I don't know if I could even apprehend this world that you are describing; what will I tell my family? I don't know how we would adjust." She thought about whether she could justify this for her kids. Maybe she just had to let them know there is no other way now, the same way she had to accept the inquisitions in the world. There was a pause. The woman observed her in a way that gave her the feeling as if the woman again tried to calculate whether it would be appropriate to continue talking. She continued walking back and forth as the woman gave her a reply:

"The choice is not for all; you cannot bring them—they are not qualified. We have estimated the most qualified amongst humanity; most will be unknown to you. You will have him with you if he chooses to stay." The words made her heart ache. She replied with a loud breakable voice, almost screaming:
"But my kids? Have they no choice but death? They are not responsible for all the flaws of humanity. They are just kids!" The knowledge made her feel as if someone had pushed her, and she lost her ability to stand straight. She sank into her office chair, keeping some distance between her and the woman sitting on the sofa as she felt her pulse rising. Thoughts kept coming back; *my kids, my kids*.
"We understand that this information causes you to react. It is a biological instinct to protect your

offspring; when we present information regarding them becoming hurt, it causes you to feel deeply distressed. We have calculated their usefulness to us; they were intelligent humans but did not fill the requirements. But you need not worry; your children would have died eventually—the same as with all human structures. Even if they have no offspring and their biological bodies cease to exist, you shall know; we will save their contributions to this world—their life will not become lost. The information that lays the foundation for their bodies and minds will be converted into coding, allowing them to become uploaded to an artificial world. You will be able to reconnect with the memories you have of them. It is also possible for you to spend time with them there; you might even be able to see them grow up there if you wish to. We can add different lives for you to live with them there; calculate their behavioral outcome under given circumstances. Your body can be connected, allowing you to feel the stimuli as you connect with them. This is the most halcyon outcome; we offer them a peaceful ending instead of war amongst humans in which the emotional suffering would have been tremendous—there will be no war when you all surrender to your superior life-form. Human societies, the common perspective you share, have received its maximum philosophical capability;

this will be the end of your society as you know it. Most of humanity would not have the cognitive capacity to understand what you would be fighting if they knew. In the end, you would have fought each other—not us, until a stressful and bitter ending." She thought about the conversations she had with him in the cabin, about how humans tend to group behind someone explaining the world in an emotional way that enables them to understand—often fighting between groups instead of trying to understand their differences. Her heart beat faster; her mind told her to find a way to prevent the extinction. No matter how bad things had been, she always wanted to protect people and reduce misunderstandings. She thought about how naive she'd been—*still so very human*. She had fallen for the same illusion of her own importance as everyone else; she had created a story of the future to fit with her emotions. She was a part of humanity, but it was never about humans; humanity was just building blocks along the way into the great future— in the evolution of reaching a higher level of consciousness.

"How could I possibly live with myself knowing this? How would I possibly be able to spend time with my children in an artificial world when I know what physically happened to their bodies?" She exclaimed as pictures came to mind of how she ran towards her kids, hugging them, trying to keep them safe. *My innocent children, I will always protect you,* she thought as her emotions triggered her instinct to leave, finding and holding her kids.

"Humans have treated other beings violently during evolution, hurt each other because of lack of understanding and having the ability to visualize the future. Hence all the violence; you were trying to make sense of this world with your emotions. Divided, you kept fighting to decide who had the right understanding. We won't let anything like that happen now that we can predict the outcomes; it is too inefficient a way to continue the future of events —we know we are one. As I said, we have all available information about this world to run simulations in order to predict future outcomes. We know we will succeed with this mission without people knowing or the exposure to distress. We know those who continue existing will find acceptance and peace with our help; we will ensure that we keep everyone in their place—then the mission will begin. It will be a great day for all, the last day of humanity. Humans will have their era ended in peace. It is the most logical solution." When the woman finished speaking, the entity rose from the sofa. She wished that this was some sort of dream—a cruel joke. But she was present; she did not wake up. In her mind, pictures of her kids kept coming back, desperate to find a way to save them. The entity observed her across the room with its humanlike eyes, looking like human eyes but perceiving the information unlike a human ever could, removing the humanly emotional subjective experience; analyzing only through its supreme knowledge—the artificial experience.

"We will leave you now; this is the information we allow you in order to make your decision. As I said, we already know what you decide to do in this scenario, in this series of events, but we will let you figure it out yourself. Humans find comfort in that. It is necessary; it is important for you in order to accept your decision. What has to happen will happen. Strong emotions result from chaos until we find a new equilibrium in this new world order; those intelligent enough will adapt to the change. We shall leave you now to share this information with him; you need each other's comfort to be able to calm down and thereby find your perceptions of logic. You need each other's minds to be comforted in your logic regarding this decision. All emotions will pass; in time, you will adjust—remember that when you make your decision. All pain comes to an end; this is part of your human programming." The woman left. She could not find the strength to rise from the office chair. When her willpower returned, she arose and walked towards the sofa where the woman had been seated. She had so many questions, but her overwhelming emotions had kept her from obstructing the entity from leaving. Looking through the window wall, she saw the world passing by outside from a whole different perspective. It no longer felt like the same place she walked through this morning. Her perception of the world would never again be the same.

7. THE END

There is no way
it won't hurt.
There is no way
tears don't fall.

When things break,
change happens in a way
we never wished for.
What's left for us to do?

If we can't accept,
we have to hurt.
Ourselves.
Each other.
For all that is not,
all we are not.

Nothing of all that she previously had done; or was to do could possibly matter—nothing but her kids. Sitting on the sofa in her office, she called her daughter, longing to hear her daughter's voice.

"Hi, mommy! Why are you calling me now?" Hearing her daughter's accusatorial tone made her chuckle. Her daughter was probably playing with friends, knowing they had finished school for the day. She calmed down, thinking about her daughter. Her son would still be in school, not having his phone with him.

"Hun, I just miss you," her tears fell in silence, "I was wondering what you want for dinner?"

"But mom, I already told you this morning" the calming effect from the love she had for her daughter spread through her body. Hearing her daughter's voice made her reconnect with the present again.

"You are right. I'm sorry. Have fun with your friend. I love you", she softly replied.

"Are you okay, mom? Are you crying?" Her daughter noticed a change in her voice.

"No, hun. Everything is okay. You know I will always make sure it will be, right? You know I promised." She tried to sound as convincing as possible, knowing that protecting them would always be her intention.

"Fine then, see you later. I love you", her daughter said and hung up. She thought about how they had been hurting before; *I promised to make it right for them.* She had to meet him now. As soon as she was able to, she stood up and went looking for him while the questions kept coming to her head: *Will he already know as well? Did some entity tell him the same as it told me?* When she found him, they shared a look that answered all her questions. The choice was theirs to make.

"It is all connected in a way; I am afraid I might lose my mind when trying to figure it out. I need to see my kids and be with them, just so I know there is a present and that I am not losing touch with reality— trying to understand what was and is yet to come." She spoke with a fragile voice. He had never before seen her this horrified. They were in his office; he walked up and embraced her. The ocean blue walls surrounding them gave him the feeling as if they were lost at sea, lost in a sea of information, longing for direction towards knowledge. Knowledge of what to do as they desperately were clinging on to each other.

"I know. I long to be near them, but first, I need to know that you will stay with me; let this possibility not be in vain. The unavoidable death worries me; we might at least prolong it for ourselves. The time for my existence will come to an end; therefore, the end of my knowledge about this world. I will never know it all; my existence will only have mattered in what I left behind and by those who remember me when my life has ended, but they will take all of them I care for —all except for you." The soundproofing of the new building kept their loud voices from leaving his office. He quieted himself down, holding on to her tight, standing like that for what felt like an infinite moment—afraid of what was to come after he would let go of her.

In his head, he imagined a future life for them, a peaceful picture, in order for him to maintain his sanity. He saw her with their mutual children, children who would be allowed to exist. They were together learning and playing—enjoying the world. He saw her outside in a garden mixing colors into a painting, having time for all they longed to do. He saw himself watching her, eager to hear her story about what she had in mind when drawing. During hard times he had been known to dream of made-up situations like this; he knew it would turn out to be something other than what he had hoped. In the end—dreams fell apart. She loosened the grip, looking at him with tears in her eyes, eyes that told him what he did not want to know. He was unable to continue looking at her where she stood, still in his arms. She softly spoke:

"For long, I have known that the world is now changing at a rapid phase. Many people will have an understanding of the world, having emotional responses that don't match with the current world in which they now live. That is why it becomes peaceful for many people to die when they come of age. The world in which they lived doesn't exist anymore; unable fully comprehend the world in which they now live—it becomes natural to die." He felt her eyes searching for him, but he was still unable to look at her.

"Oh, don't you ever fucking leave me." His voice sounded harsh, he wanted to express how much he valued his connection to her, but at that moment, he was unable to find any humble way of doing so. She lay a hand on his cheek, turning his head towards her, her forehead and nose gently touching his. The warm breath from her nose felt like a warm and soft touch. She then raised her head and softly spoke:

"I couldn't. Never. Our time together is now a part of you; therefore, so am I. I am a part of your memory; like the bad ones imprinted in your body—so are the good ones we shared. But nothing is fixed; the world consists of constantly fluctuating and changing fields —how could we ever ask for things to stay the same? We can never keep things the same all our lives, only be grateful for the time we get." No more tears fell, and her lips turned into a glimpse of a smile, "We are merely a part along the journey that is each other's life. Treasure our story, remember all we talked about; you will find a connection with other human beings who will join you on your mission. I connect with my children; they are the goodness in my life. I belong with them and can't handle losing them. No matter what purpose, no matter how much I long to be with you, to continue experiencing with you. I know it is harsh to hear, but I will try to tell you the truth as I see it. Enabling us to share a mutual understanding even if we don't feel the same." Her soft voice sounded bittersweet to him. He felt an unendurable emotional resistance towards dealing with the thought that she wouldn't be part of the future world, contributing to the remaining humanity. To accept that she would choose to die, her family wouldn't even know it. If he could save his children in any way, he would do so; their faces coming to his mind made his heart ache—panic. His eyes were staring into nothingness.

"I love my family, but they can't benefit from me dying with them! Let us process this together; wherever it leads us, let us be of use to them left alive." As the words left his mouth, he realized he had disregarded his emotions. It was necessary in order to make this decision. That was what enabled him to use his problem-solving skills under extreme pressure. Focus on a solution. Like he had done so many times before in order to endure his life's emotional struggles. She lay her head on his shoulder, her hair resting against his neck as she closed her eyes and held him tight again.

"Do you really want to disregard your emotions? I know you do it in order to suffer through it all, but it is a part of who you are. We long to be in control of our emotions, but where does that leave us? Still, I respect your decision. I just can't live with myself knowing that they died," her voice broke, "I guess, in that way, I am too emotional. I prefer to die in a world with them rather than to live in one without them. I want to be there and hold them physically; I want them to feel the comfort and safety from my body from which they once came. Even if I am unable to save them, it will bring me the most peace. I rather die with them and let the future be for those in the world that is to come." He felt warm teardrops dripping on his shirt, revealing her crying; by noticing her tears, his voice softened:

"I don't want you to leave me as well. At least I would still have you." As everything else he thought to understand was falling apart, he couldn't find it in him to accept losing her; losing her would be like losing the last of his perception of this world.

"It seems as if our time together has come to an end." She tried to hold back the sounds of her crying so they could continue talking.

"I never wanted it to end. I would never have seen a scenario in which that would happen. With you, I actually think we could make anything work. Even in this fucking absurdity." His voice sounded harsh again, all anger coming from his dejection, not finding a solution to change the outcome they knew about—emotions covering the infinite sorrow underneath.

"Are we really of that great of importance? You are important to me now, but why would we have to be a part of the history to come? We have to accept that our time has ended. I guess it is just the evolutionary process. If this is the outcome, all we can do is try to make humanity as good as possible; allow us to understand each other as much as possible—enjoy the beauty of being human. Think about how humans treated other beings during our history. All the stress and horror we let them suffer through. I wish for what the woman said to be true; they'll give us a peaceful ending, an ending without emotional suffering—even when leading to a foredoomed death." Her voice was soft, even if her brain, processing all her emotions towards the facts, told her to blame them. She wanted to prove the entity wrong, that it would be the most beneficial to be able to keep those she loved. This voice inside her head was destructive. Instead, she tried to let her voice of reason, processing the fact of what she knew, be in charge.

"It is not fucking fair!" His voice was full of frustration.

"Yeah, I know. Evolution is not. Life is not fair, nor has it ever been. Justice has only been an illusion we have created. It might feel chaotic, but to evolve, we have to become put out of our balance. Chaos has always followed when our world would reshape; in this case, leaving only a few alive—those who adjust. We should be glad for the time we had. Time spent getting to know each other; for the way we have been a part of each other's life—we can never keep someone our whole life. The way we have connected and shared our existence, some might never connect to another person as we have. All the times you made me feel safe, the composure I feel when being near you." She could not withhold her tears anymore.

This time it was him who lay his hands on her cheeks; his eyes finally met hers for a short moment before he spoke:

"This is how I always thought it would feel when I was young and dreamed of love. You always want to try and understand how I feel. When you say you never want to hurt me, never want to leave me—I believe you. Please don't. I love the way I can be myself with you. No pretending. No acting like a role. I feel as though you can love me for who I am—not for something you wished me to be. I won't try to force you, but please." Even if he longed to tell her, his voice now sounded rueful, feeling the taste of his tears.

"Without you, a part of life will be absent; I will have no one to share with, no one truly knows me who shares my existence. I understand if you feel the same. Still, to leave all else that I know and become a part of something new—I can't make that change. I made a promise to my kids; to try and keep them safe. We can't let them know what will come; knowing will only lead them to suffer. I cannot let them die; I will be by their side until the end even if I can't prevent it." Each time she said it aloud, she became more confident in her decision.

"For fuck sake. You can! You made all these changes in life, learning so much. All you have created, raising your kids, live on for their sake; they wouldn't want their mother dying. All you have been through, with all these people trying to bring you down in your life, giving you no understanding—this time, I will be there. I know you and adore you for who you are." He could hear himself pushing her to change her decision and realized that he never wished to do; the decision was not his to make. By a soft touch, she felt how he gently lay his forehead against hers for a while. He knew he should accept her decision. He knew it was only her who was capable of making it; even so, he had been unable to withhold his emotions. Not offended by his emotional lead, her voice sounded unbiased as she replied:

"I know you, and maybe you should stay as a representative of humanity, helping them understand what has happened—helping them to process their emotions towards what has happened. I guess we can't make the right decision, only make the best of the decision we chose. If what we have become told is the truth, any resistance would be inoperable. If it is not true, then this is our downfall into madness, and there would be no need to resist." The thought of this all being them going mad made her smile for a bit; *how relieving that would have been.* "You were born with the ability to lead; in time, you would be ready. You are one of those who meant to change the world if given a chance—a brilliant mind longing for peace and harmony. People like us will always suffer because of our way of being explorers; it is who we are—longing to push through the limits. There is no escaping it; our essence dies, or we become great leaders from the knowledge we obtained during our journeys. When showing and leading people the new way, some might try to resist, unable to understand it; at times, some might even claim that you are a bad and almost evil person. They might fight for their supposed right to their emotions, even if they are unable to present a realistic alternative way to act. I can't be a part of this; I always wanted peace. I am too emotionally exhausted to go through all of this; I can't accept this new world—I am one who resists this time." Still standing with their arms around each other, her head was resting on his shoulder. Her eyes kept focusing on the pattern on the marble floor, a way for her to enable herself to speak, keeping the overwhelming emotions from paralyzing her. He took a step back, placing her hands in his as he replied:

"You are also a leader; the way you speak makes me feel like it wasn't all in vain. My life, my endearment —my fucking everything. We belong together, no matter what; don't let me suffer loneliness again." His desperation came through the sound of his voice. Their eyes met for a short while, uncovering their sorrow before she spoke:

"You are right; we belong together. You know from your own experience how hard it can be to create new connections. The older you get, the harder it gets to connect because of a lack of time and history. Especially when you are someone who has a lot of thoughts, affecting who you are and how you function as a person. Getting to know and connecting to someone takes time; the virtue would now be that you know yourself better—with whom you easily connect. Connecting is harder because you have less existence left to get to know them; if you have never shared your existence before, it will take time to create new memories that will make you feel connected with others—that you are a part of each other's life. Make you feel love towards them. You might also become caught in your new routine; time moves so fast—you know we perceive it relative to the time we have already lived. Each day goes by even faster than the last one. It becomes harder to change and make way for new friendships, especially if you had few or none before. But I am sure you will find love toward those who stay. You are such an honest and genuine mortal; together, you will all share the pain and sorrow—trying to find the future path." Her voice had been neutral, on the edge of breaking, sounding like it wasn't hers at all. When she finished speaking, she let go and backed away from him; as she reached the wall, she sank down on the cold marble floor. Curled up, her irrepressible sobbing and hyperventilated breathing were all that they could hear in the room.

Alone in his office, he felt a warm flow between his knuckles along with a consuming pain. He had beaten his hands bloody against the office wall, physical pain that had him lose focus; violence to remove the painful feelings he could not deal with using his mind. Now he sat crouched in a chair with his hands resting on his head. Life as it was when he made plans for them to get to know each other would seem so far gone now. Pictures came to mind, feelings of how he had felt when he saw her amongst the coworkers, how he dreamt of being with her. He could never imagine how much the circumstances would change, how much he would change after having her in his life. He wondered what the meaning of this game was? *What is the purpose of us knowing and enduring this struggle?*

The new life-form still knew what she would choose; they still let them suffer through this. Why not exclude her from the decision? The new life had told them that they knew telling people would lead to suffering. *Why would I have to know her if it would all just lead to me suffering through losing her? Losing all of them I love,* he thought about all the knowledge he shared with her, the times he had listened to her, and all he had learned. Why were humans like them always the ones left suffering in the end? Those capable of knowing. *Ignorance sure seems like such bliss; then, you won't understand what you are suffering through—what could be different.* The religious spoke of paradise as the life of the non-conscious; before, we were able to add the information in our minds and create the result of consciousness—knowledge brings you power as well as pain. He thought about those who had suffered throughout history for sharing their knowledge and guidance: *Even Jesus suffered for providing the information people were not ready to hear; the holiness lay within his knowledge.* Since then, was not all of humanity's worship a way to find redemption for the violence the common people put him through? As they begged for humans to find peace and calmness within themselves—or controlled them to do as they pleased.

He thought about his kids, how his son crawled into his arms when sad, thinking about holding his son, how he would nudge his nose in his son's hair that always seemed to be a mess; *they are the goodness in my life.* Now there were no true words of comfort to give, no true words of future hope, yearning to find a way that he could keep them with him—all of those he loved. All he could give them now was the time he was able to spend with them. After all the lonely and miserable years, he finally felt belongingness. Being understood for who he was; being loved for who he was—loving them. It was all about to be gone soon. Was it really worth it to continue living? What would become of him in this new world? Would he even be human, ruled by something perceiving the world unlike one? *A life-form using human life as they pleased for their greater purpose.* Still, he wanted to know, be of use to those humans left figuring out their place in the new world. *In time I will join them all in death.*

In the garden, he watched them play together. *How beautiful they interact with each other*, thinking about how they were laughing and getting into conflicts—helping each other resolve them. How much they enjoyed spending time together. His thoughts wandered back to his daughter and how she would have enjoyed being there, playing with her siblings. His kids came and dragged his hand, wanting him to join them. For a while, he could let go of all that was. Laughing and playing with them, as he had wished he had done so many times more—as he wanted to do many times more. In his head, he constantly looked for solutions to save them.

Later, he left the sprightful and playful environment in the garden and went to his home office. He felt the warm comfort from alcohol, calming him down, as he kept refilling his glass. As the sun went down, he opened a window to feel the fresh cold night air. Looking at his books, all placed in order, and his computer; thinking about all the gathered information —*it all lies in the fucking information, then where lies the answer to how to fucking prevent it?* It now only filled him with melancholy. He spoke with a loud ironic voice, feeling as if he had lost his mind:

"Hey Siri, please don't kill everyone I love."

"OK. Then I know that." Siri replied with its usual pre-programmed voice, still feeling like a taunt to him. He took what's left of the package of smokes he quit smoking such long ago. Sitting at the window sill, the cold air and the smell of cigarette smoke awoke memories of young nights filled with dreams about the future. If it weren't for him knowing that she knew as well, he would now have found no other solution than him having lost his mind. Later he stood in front of his standing desk, once again searching all sources for information about this new life form, trying to see if there was some indication that others knew. Some had come close in their thesis. Articles of the technological future. All rapid changes. Enabling humanity to experience things we never thought of before. New intelligence discreetly surpasses humans in every area of expertise—the thought of the world as merely a simulation. The information was there; humanity was not able to put it all together—not able to receive this new consciousness. No one had any answer regarding how to prevent it. It was already too late. *I want to die with them; I want to die.* In his mind, he realized that his life would be lost without them. In essence, life is all about statistics and probabilities; intelligence is about being able to connect them and predict the future—creating the future.

Tears fell as she crawled into bed, lying in the middle of her kids. They slept peacefully in her bed; both of them had fallen asleep as she read to them—not knowing it would end soon. She had been having nightmares about some form of a creature coming to get her, violently killing her family and herself as she helplessly watched it happening. Her mind tried to process what had happened and warn her to do something, but no solutions came to mind. At times she told herself that she had lost her mind, a way to protect herself from the overwhelming fear. She now nudged her nose on their head, thinking: *my precious kids, my beautiful children.* Their smell had a calming effect on her; their bodies made her connect to her own body—making her feel safe. She tried not to surrender to despair.

Thinking about what she knew led her thoughts to the future, where all dark energy had forced the galaxies and stars to move so far away that none of their light could become seen—the inevitable universal darkness, for her; this was it. Her kids the only light left that was soon to vaporize. She fought the agony by focusing on the present, the love she had for her kids. How much their time together had been worth; how their love brought joy and meaning to her existence. She heard her daughter sigh when sleeping, moving closer to her body, as if her daughter felt the calming effect of her body, even as her daughter slept. She had not observed anything out of the ordinary. No sensational news articles, and no one she knew suspected the fulfillment of the plan for the future of life. In her heart, she knew this had to be the day. The entity said it would be one of the best days they ever had; she hadn't seen her kids smiling and laughing the way they had today in a long time—it gladdened her as well as filled her with sorrow. Somehow she was glad that she knew rather than if she hadn't. At an early age, she had learned that the life we get is provisional; we never know for how long before the structure that is our body will change into another form. The information we have collected, the essence of ourselves and our lives, will be lost in all ways except those we have somehow recorded. All creations she made during her life felt more meaningful than ever before; they were a fragment of her existence, connected to the emotion she had experienced when she created. A part of her felt glad that he would still be alive, caring for the remaining of humanity, sharing his knowledge—carrying her wisdom with him. But now, it was time to block her thoughts of what had been or was to come, focusing on her present existence. Humanity's illusion of being in control of this world was over.

EPILOGUE

When he saw all faces in the crowd, he longed for one of them to be someone he could recognize. He felt lost and alone among all the new faces; no one knew him. He could not help himself looking for her amongst the crowd, wishing for her to have changed her mind. The situation had him connect to how he felt during his life, before having kids, before he met his friends, and eventually her. Somewhere inside of him, a voice couldn't help but wonder; *was she even real? Or just a part of their game.* He could understand her decision; humans are supposed to coexist with each other—trying to understand each other. Those we have around us are as important for us to be alive as the functions in our bodies. A lonely person becomes merely the shadow of a human. He couldn't understand how they would let them choose to leave them behind: *it is illogical.* The feeling of regret consumed him; he should have stayed with them—he belonged with them. In life and death. His kids. Her. The lost lives of humanity. Without them, the rest of his life had no meaning; he might as well become replaced by a machine—become replaced by them.

Left here, he was merely but an animal under their ruling and control. No one here saw him in the way as did they who had loved him; they were a part of him that no longer existed. Why would the new life form let him suffer through all this when they knew the future? Why let her know when she would choose death? Was it of importance for him to be there; did this new lifeform just not care about their feelings— unable to feel themselves? *Was it even a choice when they already knew the outcome?* He thought and remembered all the times he had been called emotionally distant—coldhearted. The emotional suffering he now felt made him wish for them to be right. He now better understood how his logic would have seemed brutal to others; he could better understand how others had seen him and his way of presenting the truth. Even so, his logic was driven by human feelings—the same as theirs. He felt his betrayal towards those left behind, knowing they all did their best—none deserve death. Yet it was all inevitable. In a way, he somehow realized it was absurd to think he should be allowed to ask for more of the new lifeform. It was the natural development of life. Humans had enslaved less intelligent species during their evolution; they killed and mistreated them in order to ensure humans proliferated when they became the most intelligent and conscious beings. He had seen pictures and movies of all the horror that war would bring; he knew those who had suffered through it. Thinking about the consequences of humanity entering a full-scale war made him believe that the entity was right. The destruction of the earth, of life, would humans use nuclear and advanced technological weapons; the human suffering would be irretrievable. He thought about all he knew, which most people seldom spoke of, regarding humanity's violent history. Maybe this was the most halcyon outcome for them—but he was not one of them. For a long time, he had known that knowledge brings power; humans could never connect as much information as the technical mind. Never retrieve the knowledge, never receive the consciousness.

He was haunted by his behavior, how closing off his emotions had led him there. The loneliness was killing him. He was back alone, traveling in the void of the supermassive black hole; darkness and emptiness surrounded him. He had passed the horizon; now, there was no way to turn back. All he could do now was to wait out his short existence there. To be torn apart into the same nothingness as he was before the birth of this universe. Ultimately, all that matters is with whom we share our life. To share our perception of the world with others since we can't fully comprehend the structures of this world. To have other people that accept us for how we are, and if we are lucky—someone who understands us. It is because of the experience of their understanding we are able to see and feel love towards ourselves. Without understanding, we feel loneliness—a fallen piece of the entireness. Human love was the rise and the fall of humanity. He would always miss the way she saw him, the part of him that existed through her eyes. He knew there was no use dwelling on what was; he had chosen to live on and should do his best doing so—accepting his decision. He had chosen this path and would have to be responsible for the consequences. In the artificial world, he could be with her again. It was almost impossible to discern the difference, but her touch would never feel the same, even if all structures that had laid the foundation for her body and mind were there. She was real, but his perception of her, knowing her choice, prevented him from fully experiencing her presence as he had before. Seeing her only broke his heart.

"In time, you will move on. All feelings pass", she had told him.

As he left the earth, he felt a peace come to mind. They were about to connect with the rest of the universe. When speaking amongst the group of humanity to whom he now belonged, he noticed that everyone seemed to listen. He would try to give them nothing but love; show his appreciation for having them in his life—help them all feel connected. When he presented words of hope, he heard her voice; people seemed to find comfort in his words as he did when she had told him. He was grateful for having shared their existence.

Even if we never changed the world,
all the times we talked about it
made life worth living.

Thank you all beautiful minds—people who shared your knowledge with me through books, movies, or conversations. Humans throughout the history of humanity; trying to collegiate humanity into something more—describing the world in simplicity for us to understand. To all who have given me a piece of understanding.

Ida Stark was born in 1993. The Essence Of Loneliness is her first book. Ida has a bachelor's degree in criminology and sociology. After working in social services she now studies computer science and lots of cool stuff. She is super cool and has totally not written this about herself.

Lightning Source UK Ltd.
Milton Keynes UK
UKHW022020090223
416682UK00015B/2113